MW01286969

The Book of C

"Building slowly but progressively and replete with unexpected everything, *The Book of Colors* is nothing less than purely original and brilliantly written."
   Manhattan Book Review

"You'll hear Yslea's voice long after you've stopped reading. … A brave novel, popping with hope."
   The Charlotte Observer

"A life-affirming novel about love and second chances"
   Publishers Weekly

"Yslea is a keen-eyed young woman with a wandering mind who picks up on fine details of the little things of life…. A beautifully written debut."
   BOOKLIST

"In the traditions of Toni Morrison and Flannery O'Connor, Raymond Barfield presents a gorgeous and dismaying human tapestry from the edges of Southern society. … An ethereal story of poverty and redemption that ends with a phoenix-like flourish and abounds with grace."
   Foreword Reviews

"Yslea's world is small, but it embraces an immense universe of wonderments, bright emotions, slant thoughts and patterns that only she can discover. In *The Book of Colors* Raymond Barfield reveals a story like no other I have experienced, inexorably dark in circumstance but triumphantly luminous in spirit. 'We are made up of pieces but somehow we feel whole.' That wholeness is celebrated in these brave pages. They seized upon me like an angelic visitation. What a wonderful novel!"

Fred Chappell, past North Carolina Poet Laureate

"I just finished *The Book of Colors*. I cried at the end, which I almost never do, not because it was sad but because it was so sweet and clear and beautifully written ... different in a really wonderful way."

Cathy Langer, The Tattered Cover bookstore

"I was lucky enough to see the first draft of *The Book of Colors*, and the beautiful strength of both the author and the main character has stayed with me a very long time. Kudos to Unbridled for bringing two powerful voices to light."

Carl Lennertz

Dreams and Griefs of an Underworld Aeronaut

"These brilliantly crafted poems inhabit a rich space where experience, psyche, myth, and the gem of language intersect. Raymond Barfield invites us to the soulful journey C. G. Jung imagined when he wrote, Everything living strives for wholeness. In reading *Dreams And Griefs Of An Underworld Aeronaut* we travel beside this poet mindfully searching and pointing beyond by way of his art, grief, faith, and love."

Rachel Blum

"Raymond Barfield writes that he just needs 'room, air, and the unknown,' but his collection gives us this, and far more. These poems pulse in their textured, sensual language, creating a world chromatic and incantatory, brooding with 'puppets, shadows and tales,' tangible and elusive at the same time. These poems draw us in and give us breath."
   Brian Swann

"Raymond Barfield circles us through hell in a hot air balloon that doubles as an Italian bagpipe blowing through ecstatic nights of betrayal's rave. The poet is back to escort us through a nightmare path in chocked terza rima sonnets while a mad dog howls at the moon and a gargoyle croons in the background. Barfield gnaws his pen into flame on the darkness of the white page to perform transfusions that translate hymns of Ars Signorum into your mind. These poems take you there. It is up to you to come back."
   Kevin Gallagher

"In this wonderful book, Raymond Barfield draws inspiration from the narrative terza rima of Dante and from the compressions and turns of the sonnet form to compress his meditations on life, pain, love, and death into 15-line poems that amaze with their range of feelings and their turns of language. The emotional depths and verbal surprises pull the reader forward through Barfield's fascinating layers of worlds and underworlds."
   John Bensko

Life in the Blind Spot

"Ray Barfield's poems are hot ice, metaphor and metaphysics. His style is beautifully controlled and then he lets go at just the right moment. Wonderful."
  Katia Kapovich

"Raymond Barfield's poems are essential to the age we live in. These philosophically searching, lucidly sensual poems drive at the heart of our understanding. With mindful grace, and 'suspecting / more than the world to be the case', Barfield brings to mind our sense of 'the variations of history', the many signs and moments that flicker and converge in the various single flame of our existence."
  Ben Mazer

"You just have to read one poem... 'Driving'...to realize that Raymond Barfield is a great American poet. You read other poems and you realize that he is more than that. You put the book down and wonder how you ever lived without it."
  Joe Green

Wager: Beauty, Suffering, and Being in the World

"You do not have to read this book, but I wager if you do, you will discover you are very glad you did. It is a book of wisdom written by a person who refuses to let how they think we should think and live be determined by disciplinary boundaries. I have a sense this book may become a classic."
  Stanley Hauerwas, Gilbert T. Rowe Professor Emeritus of Divinity and Law, Duke University

"Here you will find everything we have come to expect from this extraordinary philosopher, physician, musician, and teacher. Subtle arguments, philosophical erudition, and probing questions are all clothed in a warm and accessible style. We are made to think as perhaps never before about that ultimate risk, the 'wager' on God, and the questions that we all send heavenward at some time or another: 'Are you there?' and 'What if you are there?'"

Jeremy Begbie, Duke University and the University of Cambridge

"Raymond Barfield has written a beautiful, compelling, and absorbing book. What makes it so special is that it is written with intellectual sophistication and yet carries the smooth, satisfying prose of a novelist; that it is fun and engaging and yet addresses the greatest subject of all; that it is inspired by a great apologist from four hundred years ago but is as contemporary as could be. This is a marvelous writer wrestling with the reader, with himself, and ultimately with God: and giving each a profound blessing."

Sam Wells, Vicar, St. Martin-in-the-Fields

The Seventh Sentence

Raymond Barfield

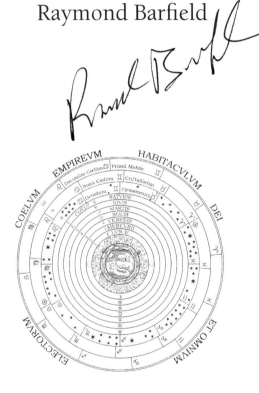

SPUYTEN DUYVIL
New York   Paris

Library of Congress Cataloging-in-Publication Data

Names: Barfield, Raymond, 1964- author.
Title: The seventh sentence / Raymond Barfield.
Description: New York ; Paris : Spuyten Duyvil, [2023]
Identifiers: LCCN 2022053660 | ISBN 9781959556046 (paperback)
Classification: LCC PS3602.A77536 S48 2023 | DDC 813/.6--dc23
LC record available at https://lccn.loc.gov/2022053660

For Donald Phillip Verene,
and for everyone lucky enough to drink excellent
whiskey with him
in the Vico Library
while pronouncing thunderwords
from Joyce's
Finnegans Wake

"garbage has to be the poem of our time because/garbage is spiritual, believable enough//to get our attention . . ."
   A.R. Ammons, *garbage*

"Oh tell me how to cure myself of irony, the gaze that doesn't penetrate."
   Adam Zagajewski, *Mysticism for Beginners*

"I want a new drug."
   Huey Lewis and the News

1. Die Welt ist alles, was der Fall ist.

He read aloud, his tongue thickened by alcohol, his voice glogged by peanut butter residue:

"Deipnosophistae. 1.5. The sea perch, the turbot, the fish with even teeth and with jagged teeth, must not be sliced, else the vengeance of the gods (*else the vengeance of the gods*) may breathe upon you. Rather bake and serve them whole, for it is much better so."

The girls, down below, on the beach, walked, unaware of the place they had in the mind and philosophical imagination of the one abandoned and untapped by Providence, ignored by the higher guardians of the verities.

"The wriggling polyp (*the wriggling polyp*), if it be

rather large, is much better boiled than baked, if you beat it until tender (*beat it until tender*)."

Into the delicious chasm of the girls' sensuous but lugubrious presence in the universe he poured ideas about beauty as a portal, a veritable passage, populated on its moist and cave-like walls with a cornucopia of images translating voluptuous darkness into eternal truth, but with his advanced intellect he did so in a way that would doubtless be inaccessible to their cute little minds.

"As for the red mullet, that will give no strength to the glands (*strength to the glands*). For she is a daughter of the virgin (*daughter of the virgin*) Artemis, and loathes rising passion (*loathes rising passion*). Again the scorpion—may it creep up and take a bite out of your buttocks (*bite out of your buttocks*)."

He looked down upon the girls with philosophical calmness, at long last bereft of active desire. "Silphium-stalks and ox-hides, they don't write philosophy like that anymore!" said Simeon Saint-Simone, Doctor of Philosophy—almost. He was consigned to that absurd, but modestly honorable, limbo called All But Dissertation, ABD, skipping the letter C (comedic, cursed, etc.), since he never finished, or to be exact, never started the ludicrous exercise of tracking down every known fact related to some irrelevant singularity in history, some obscure dullard who, just because he wrote a few words in Greek and happened to have been dead for 2000ish years, was labeled a philosopher—a *philosopher* who would have been despised and dismissed and told to go do something useful like repairing chariots if ever he met Ludwig Wittgenstein. Good old LW, the intellectual and spiritual briar patch in which Simeon's magnificent mind tangled itself, making it impossible for him to ever finish a thought.

Besides, what does that even mean, *finishing a thought*? When one is in a battle with Providence, sometimes one must simply submit and enjoy the tumbling adventure, trusting that something wonderful will come to pass, as it had with Simeon Saint-Simone, when the entire effort to devise that monstrosity of literary mediocrity, the dissertation, was transformed into a sublime work he called *The Garden of Memory*. Had there ever been a dissertation other than LW's *Tractatus Logico-Philosophicus* that could show forth the world, all that is the case, as did Simeon's Garden, with touch both grave and persiflageous?

Virtue, developed by long habit, had allowed him to escape the philosophy department when The Chair of Philosophy, after a periphrastic demonstration of non-linear, non-logical admonitions, finally got to the point and said that other students were complaining that he did not bathe often enough, and that he stunk up the seminar room in an apparently distracting way that did not even evoke references to the great Cynic, Diogenes, within the truncated intra-cranial swirls they called minds. He had put aside the iron chain of his unfinished Doctor of Philosophy and had resumed his singular brand of contemplation, keeping the fabric of wisdom intact, almost certainly the only person in America, or the universe for that matter, who was mining the works of Athenaeus for culinary ideas while sensing the glory emanating from the Garden of Memory.

His was a mind set apart, hovering sublimely above thick cracked glasses held together with a strip of duct tape, a dirty undershirt clinging tightly just above his umbilicus, and worn slippers indenting the flesh of his edematous feet far below.

Simeon lay mostly-naked on a used cardiology tilt-table in the house of his childhood.

He sipped ouzo from a heavy, gold-rimmed crystal goblet he gripped with his moist, doughy hand. As he pondered the possibility of Absolute Knowledge in an age of store-bought optimism he watched a trickle of sweat originating from some glandular depth roll down the exposed part of his vast and unmystical belly, landing in the pool of his navel. He pushed aside the stray strands of thinning hair blown onto his face in a gust from the sea, and he lifted his ouzo to his magnificent nostrils, filling them with the spirit of bitterness.

Now in middle age he found cordials of aniseed and wormwood more satisfying, and less expensive, than the scotch he once favored, a shift of taste that better fit the dwindling coffers supporting his philosophical life, though it was a shift that did not diminish his craving for high-priced prawns provoked by his Loeb Edition of *Sophists at Dinner*. A great drop of sweat fell from the tip of his nose into the goblet, leaving a cloudy streak in the glass.

In one swallow he drank half the ouzo to clear the viscous slime remaining from his night of sleep that had been repeatedly punctuated with attacks of apnea when physiologically sinister relaxation forced his tongue and pharynx to cave in on themselves, blocking the passage of breath and transforming somnolent repose into a never-ending battle with his own flesh. As the warmth spread through his 389 pounds he felt some solid and unmovable truth beckoning to him from every direction—from the icons flaking gold and leaning against the wall next to his tilt-table; from the frail and ancient lion wandering among the heaps of clean waste and discarded junk piled all around the gated yard of his sea-side mansion; and from his Cuban Gardener, Jerome, the librarian of eternal longing, keeper of the secret, the one who, whenever he finally decided to wake up and start earning his pay, never failed to look toward Simeon from the Garden with eyes concealed by shadows, as doleful as the eyes of a cow biding time in the pasture.

How his loins rejoiced at the gathering of an early morning shower outside his open window, a sweet rain enlivening love and yearning, as the earth is enlivened and the sea is made to swell.

He surveyed the Garden of Memory, the work of his life, recording the demise of humanity in order to become the birth of its renewal. No one—except, perhaps, Jerome—saw what he saw in the carefully arranged mosaic of discard.

Axiom: *thought must mingle with the lower world for a new object to become part of the res.*

Evidence: tupperware bowls require the mind's intent to achieve their diameter and their color. Toothpaste, mentholatum, and anti-nausea suppositories all require the bearing down of thought. When they are used, and their purposes accomplished, there yet remains the residuum, the husk of discarded form, in which one can see the remnant of the first thought that brought it into existence—the toothpaste tube, say. And yet consider the accumulation of discarded toothpaste containers.

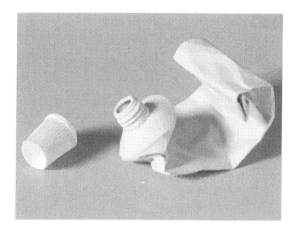

Simeon pulled out a sheet of paper to calculate, roughly, the meaning, in physical terms, of this residuum. But he quickly tired of the task. He was constitutionally inclined toward the universal rather than the details of a particular calculation that was the work of banks, Scrooges, and whores.

In another swallow he drank the second half of the ouzo and allowed his blue eyes to gaze lovingly toward the bodies of the young women scattering beneath his feet as the rain established itself. The rain flowered and, amidst the panic of squeals, emptied the beach of the virginal and non-virginal alike.

Some minds move by a slow, stepwise mechanism of discursive thought. Simeon's was tilted toward the wrenching insight that inverts the world and breaks lesser men, the touching of eternity from inside the bungled finitude of our bodies. And so, he knew the squeals were disingenuous, cargoes of lies, like all expressions of the young, dimly veiling sex. He also understood weather, as he understood the patterns of humanity. After twenty years of looking out his window toward the sea, sipping ouzo, and reclining upon the tilt-table, Simeon knew the feel of a quickly passing rain.

While the timid hovered under awnings and umbrellas, Simeon put down his Loeb and turned his mind to a single numbered sentence from Ludwig Wittgenstein's *Tractatus Logico-Philosophicus*. For a few moments he savored it, feeling for the structured and strained clarity of Ludwig's inward being. Reading even a single sentence from the soul of LW gave him hope that he might one day distill *The Idea of the Garden* into a book. The language of the *TL-P* was not Simeon's language, because his own mind was balanced atop the flesh of a massive body, while LW's body was lean, ascetic, even sickly. Simeon was of a port, expansive if stained and dandruffy, but he knew that he too was capable of completing a work even though, like everything ultimately, he morosely supposed, it would end in silence.

Ludwig's *Tractatus* was not the only important *Tractatus* in the library of Simeon's mind. There was another one that Providence leveraged in order to bring Jerome the Cuban into his life. Jerome and Simeon were at the yard sale of the recently widowed spouse of a retired Latin professor, and both of them were looking at books on a table marked *Free*. Jerome, who looked like a homeless man, because he was homeless, opened an over-documented dissertation by one of the professor's students on Ramon Lull's *Liber ad memoriam confirmandam*.

Simeon eyed the book while Jerome turned the pages, and behold: in the wasteland of fussy erudition they simultaneously paused at a little paragraph speculating about Lull's insistence that a person who wanted to strengthen his memory must use another of Lull's books containing an absolutely essential clue—*The Book of the Seven Planets*. Unfortunately, the tedious student pointed out in a self-satisfied footnote lacking all sense of wonder, Lull never wrote a book by this title. More fortunately, the slightly less tedious following sentence noted, Lull did write a book called *Tractatus de Astronomia* in which he suggested that memory must be based on the celestial *seven*.

"Ha! This," Simeon pointed out to the tall and gloomy Jerome, "is today's treasure! A clue!"

Jerome nodded but did not smile. What else could such a response lead to except Jerome's employment as curator of the Garden? The memory of this evoked a brief stab of nostalgia, which was quickly replaced by the idea of writing a new treatise called *Tractatus Gastronomicus* mirroring the book of the seven planets, but with continual reference to the globes of the body—the breasts, the testicles, the ovaries, the kidneys, the heart, and the stomach—all the organs of desire chomping life beneath the dismayed gaze of the seventh globe, the brain, sometimes staring with a rarified horror, and sometimes with the omental lunge toward unappeasable desire, Quasimodo ogling Esmeralda whose shimmering presence disclosed the infinity of erotic impossibility.

He poured another glass of ouzo to temper the strained meandering of his thought. While he waited for the rain to pass, he put aside the *Tractatus* and picked up the advertisements for locally sold junk, the artifacts of the *Fall*, to search for additions to his Garden of Memory. If he ever did write a book revealing the secret of the Garden, perhaps the title should be simpler—something elegant like *The Idea* or maybe just *Idea*.

The breeze cleaned by the rains brushed against his massive body, reminding him simultaneously of his own frailty and his desire for eternal life, mixed with his desire for primal odors like those of roasted ox-chine.

"Acorns of Zeus!" he thought. "Why is the odor of roasted ox-chine no longer smelled on city streets?"

The white shrimp boats creeping out to sea were barely visible through the rain. He had a symbolic and symbiotic relationship with the shrimpers. In a storm they might feel the pressure of weather and need. These were raw facts. But Simeon Saint-Simone understood the meaning of the facts. Together they shared the secret of the weather. The facts, and the meaning of the facts, the musical notes and the silences between the notes that are also music, the music of silence, the silence of music, the Museless musings, a-musing as a trifling but non-trivial negation.

As he had predicted by smell and feel, the rain quickly subsided and the beach was soon a writhing organism absorbing the life-and-melanoma-giving warmth of the sun, covered with gorgeous corpuscles, each a young, firm body.

He swallowed the last of his ouzo. The bottle was empty. His delight plateaued, and he was as Agamemnon reviled by Achilles, heavy with wine, whose eyes were those of a dog.

Because he was hidden by the glare of the morning sunlight on the open window's screen, he had the opportunity to consume the smorgasbord of human variety, and to gaze freely upon the proudly displayed and scarcely-clad breasts and genitals, the fount of the new world giving hope, among other things, to old men—those for whom the youthful illusion of time had been utterly replaced by the time of the Laundromat, where things are accomplished, order is established, and cleanliness is made available to the least of these, in the midst of a very specific kind of space and time, full of the sounds of purposeful mechanism, the push-pull click of machines that only take metal money, the sameness of color on the walls, machines, and plastic chairs, the folding of underwear in front of strangers, the abandon that is non-pornographic, merely human, with holes and wornness as exposed as our desire to be clean, ordered, and fresh, escaping the clots and mud pits of mortal life, if only for the hour bought by eight quarters.

Philosophical experience had also made him suspicious of such ravings, because sometimes he suspected it was not his magnificent mind that was raving, but rather the thinking and blathering twin he had resorbed while still in his mother's womb. His suspicion was a form of humility, but because he was inhabited by more than one voice, he became, without pretension, a world, a veritable summation of decay and hope.

His lifework was to refine the Carpocratian insight

that by testing all vices he might gain experience, and through this experience gain wisdom. By becoming the receptacle of all waste and rubbish he was surreptitiously approaching the point of cultural salvation, conquering all by consuming all—all brands of cigarettes, the vapidest of pornography, the thinnest of plots in poorly written novels, and the most nonchalant of philosophies abandoning humanity to its ruin. He rehearsed aloud the poetry of the wines of Galen, wines that moistened the lungs. Falerian, Trifolian, Buxentine, and Velitern ... Caecuban, Nomentan, Trebellic, and Iotaline. His life was a reverie, the reverie of consumption. And he was very nearly happy.

His mind achieved coherence. The chant of lists regressed. The garbage from TV and the rubbish from magazines receded. Even the barbarism prophesied by the great Giambattista Vico dispersed, sort of. Distraction—the constant background droning that humanity has yet to understand—hummed, of course. But this is why only a truly *great* mind is capable of subsuming the whole until barbarism is tamed and the unacknowledged horror of the varieties of detergent on the grocery store shelf, available and screeching for the consumer's attention, is made into the language of *The Idea Itself* through the alchemy of the great brain, a brain such as

Simeon Saint-Simone's, moving toward the pinnacle attested to by Aristotle in *De Caelo*, and by Thomas in the first part of the great *Summa* in question 77, article 2, sed contra: *The highest perfection is found in those things which acquire perfect goodness without any movement whatever*. Simeon, naked on his tilt-table, was acquainted with the taste of this particular kind of perfection.

Now and only now, he concluded tentatively, was he ready for love.

He pulled a new bottle of ouzo from the small refrigerator beside his tilt-table, and he refilled his glass.

Disdain for transience has no place in the optimistic reach of an inventor's mind toward a fine idea such as toothpaste. And yet the inevitability of being discarded is embedded in the instantiation of such an idea, like the foul streak of Satan staining the purity of virgins. Upon this heap of rubbish Simeon bent his mind, feeling his way toward a redemptive thought that would save mankind from barbarism. From his home in vaguely mythical Florida with its crocodile farms, oranges, Cubans, old people, swamps, and condos susceptible to a Venetian fate if climate change is true, he was compelled to cry out with Ramon Fernandez, *Tell me, if you know. Oh! Blessed rage for order, pale Ramon, the maker's rage to order words of the sea, words of the fragrant portals, dimly-starred, and of ourselves and of our origins, in ghostlier demarcations, keener sounds.* In fact, Florida even looked a bit like Italy.

The phone startled him and cold ouzo sloshed onto his pale chest with its few gray hairs scattered across the vastness. The answering machine came on and he heard his own voice, a bored, husky baritone speaking only the seven digits of his number, followed by a piercing beep.

Someone, a girl with a voice that sounded too young to say anything that could possibly interest Simeon, began to blather without making any immediate point. If there was an end to her sentences, it emerged from her mouth with an improper and annoying upward inflection, making each declarative sentence a half-question.

Then the mumbling voice dropped to a whisper and the machine mercifully cut it off.

He sipped his ouzo and regained the mental composure necessary for his work. He had heard this voice before. Generally, he did not clutter his mind with the memories of other people's voices and peculiarities, though his memory was capacious. But that upward inflection at the end was a barb, and it caught on his hippocampus.

The phone rang again.

He moaned as he emptied his glass.

The same girl's voice clawed at his inner ear. He had definitely heard this voice before.

"Simeon, your father is dead." In the following silence the phone cut her off.

"Ah, yes!" He emptied the second ouzo bottle into his crystal goblet with some satisfaction and lifted it to his fleshy, bluish lips. "Augusta. That was Augusta."

The shrimpers were now far from shore, and farther still was the shipping lane where tankers passed, carrying goods to and from nations that had been enemies in the not-too-distant past, until the possibility of profit disrupted the manly, but dissipating, art of war. Simeon toasted the gods of commerce and their ludicrous foundation for peace.

All was well. He was safely ensconced, a piece of debris left over in the wake of the American Dream, making a home among the discarded forms of convenience items, preparing for a thought.

The truly great thought is rare, the one that goes beyond the useful item or the delineation of physical fact, requiring the harvesting of all human memory, squeezing from it the essential intellectual energy in the way creatures draw life-energy from the superfluity of the sun's burning of itself toward eventual oblivion. The problem was that he quickly bored himself when his mind ballooned into *the truly great thought*. Maybe his mind was distracted by the concreteness of the ten-thousand small, discarded facts in his Garden of Memory that kept the eye seeking and the mind agile, curious. Maybe the great idea went suddenly flaccid because he tried to say it prematurely. Unfortunately, no matter when it was said, it would be premature, making it difficult to say indeed. Especially for one who would die. Ah, death, threshold of mystery, portal of uncanniness, cauldron of horror, blah blah blah.

As he settled back into the dark chorus emanating from the mouthy fangs that hovered on the periphery of his well-being, the phone rang yet again, awakening a dash of dread. Augusta's girlish voice became more insistent. "I am coming to your house. I will be there this afternoon. We need a funeral feast. I hope no one is injured, or killed."

While she spoke, he struggled to roll off his tilt-table and get to the phone so he could say, firmly, *No!* But she was gone before both of his feet were on the ground.

He lay back again on the tilt-table and adjusted his naked genitals below his magisterial belly. He picked up a rag that he kept with his ouzo and cigarettes on a small table, and he wiped the sweat from his face, big as a buffalo's. The day went dull, transformed by the will of another into a gray slather against the background collage of light rays and the hum of squeaky teenage voices. He smoked more rapidly and blew the smoke from his vast nostrils in noisy exhalations. The veil keepers were uncharacteristically busy hiding the scaffolding of joy upon which hung the tent of meaning in the universe.

He felt the uncomfortable pull of an old panic as he looked over toward the mirror on the wall, glaring at his thick lips, his great navel, the calluses where his belly rubbed against his trousers.

So, apparently his father was dead.

Simeon resumed staring at the maritime navels of the girls on the beach. He looked down at his own. His was cavernous and linty. He could not say which type of navel was better for the purposes of contemplation. Different sorts of thoughts arose depending on the appearance of the navel. The small, perfect navel inclined him toward sunny thoughts, thoughts of a merry, practical, productive, or even reproductive nature, not that he was in any way drawn to ephebophilia, for he was not a philiac of any kind. His own navel, which had once been tethered to that mediating organ, the placenta, through which he first negotiated life with his mother, yielded dark thoughts, damp-cave thoughts, melancholia felt against the mental hum of chaos, and the loss of an elusive, allusive, illusive control over beginnings, middles, and ends.

Self-knowledge did not relieve the panic creeping through the private shadows of his inner world without his permission. *Why, why this disruptive panic?* He already carried the responsibility of his own selfless rehearsal of unredeemable rubbish, which was his gift to a culture drowning in words and garbage, and humping one another promiscuously all the way down the garbage shoot. *But is it really so bad?* Look at the kids playing on the beach with their smooth skin and perfect bodies. How thoroughly he wished to dilate on the virtues of women. He might be hounded by the condominium builders on either side of his home who hated his Garden of Memory because of the impact on property value, but this was his place, his physical portal into the truth of the whole, which, admittedly, manifested itself in garbage-laden patterns that were the physical form of a strangely lugubrious poetic wisdom.

He reached down for another bottle of ouzo. The bottles were so thin.

He raised his glass to the two bigger-than-life saints painted on the large wooden panels next to his tilt-table, and he continued to sip rather than guzzle, a gesture, a veritable proof of his self-control.

His saints had such refined looks of peace in the midst of exquisite pain. He toasted them. "My God, folks, at times like this I could almost believe." The ancient emptiness of his house absorbed his slightly slurred confession: "Perhaps I do believe."

Water dripped from his gutters. All the wet world was alive, hoisting its flesh and fur from slumber, and calling out to the pleasantly drunk and elevated Simeon Saint-Simone, urging him to continue his search for truth as he made his heart glow with absinth, and felt the pull of Phosphorus and the Dog-star, hidden by sunlight, hidden by all the gratuitous excess of light.

Augusta. The thought of her invaded his pursuit of the veil keepers. He surrendered in a puff of smoke from his Lucky Strikes, hoping to toss the thought to the side using its own momentum.

He met her only once, seven years before, at his mother's funeral. He was late, so he did not sit with the family. Not that there was room enough for his girth in the two reserved rows. He crept up the side aisle next to the great cathedral wall and hid behind a column, skulking left and right around the pillar, feeling the faintest echoes from the distant past when, under a sky that did not reach much higher than the mountains, monastic choirs sang to a purposeful God. His mother's gray pate poked out above the coffin's edge, she whose womb was his anteroom to the world of material things, a womb already on its way to the very decay that would one day be his doorway out of the world of material things and into the rarified world of abstract entities, or else the even more rarified world of annihilation.

Augusta-the-frail was sitting next to the old man on the front pew of the church, occupying—just barely because of the near absence of matter filling out her form—the place of honor.

Augusta. Augusta-of-the-Shadows . . . How to remember the pieces, the fragments in his mind's memory theater where she had a greenish tinge to her hair, hair that was thin and breakable, hair that might come out if rubbed too hard. The green color was not factually accurate. But there it was anyway. In his memory. Her skin wrapped around her like a sheet of phyllo dough, sickly and transparent. Her limbs were wonders of insubstantiality. When she stood up at the end of the service, he noticed that the triangular space between her inner thighs, which would normally give his loins a thrill, was out of proportion to the thickness of her legs and pelvis, leaving him with the unfortunate impression of a walnut cracker.

None of this illuminated the mystery of why, amidst the boiled paleness of her warm evocation of death, there was also something philosophically erotic about her. His mind floated toward her like a hot air balloon in windless conditions, drifting slowly toward the front of the cathedral. The confluence of death, desire, angels, and angles ineluctably raised, within his well-trained mind, the image of the erotic monk, Abelard, and his Heloise in Notre-Dame, where she was seduced inside the walls of her uncle Fulbert's house, yielding a son she named *Astrolabias*, after the scientific instrument, immediately suggesting to the moist and pliant ground of Simeon's fertile brain the slight etymological detour from the name of an early sextant used to measure the angular distance among celestial objects, to the image of astrolabium, celestial lips, no less fixed among heavenly angles. Yes, a considerable improvement over the pedestrian comparison with a walnut cracker.

Providence extended no more favors at the actual burial, and he was forced to sit next to Augusta because of the funeral director's grossly polite pushiness. The foul and knavish director, who was not a thin man, refused to let him stand anonymously on the periphery. All eyes were drawn to his awkward obesity. Obesity: that which does not fit into chairs, that which spills from the sides, that which crowds the elevator, that which lays down silver-gray stretch marks on pink skin, that which thickens skin, staining the inner thighs and armpits. He thus despised the funeral director and his flimsy folding chairs with slipcovers embroidered with his initials, the undertaker's gaudy grasp after immortality among the dressing up of love and rot. His trousers were uncomfortably tight, constricting his thighs and calves and genitals. Because of the recent rain, the air was wet and sticky, and he was hungry. All of this pressed in on his waning patience. And then, though it was not written into the funeral plan, his father spontaneously decided that his mother's body should be lowered in the presence of all, and that the grave should be filled with dirt before anyone left.

Tormentor.

Simeon watched the womb in which he had been conceived levitate on the belts as they lowered his mother into the ground. The sound of dirt and pebbles landing on her coffin evolved into the muted thud of mere dirt on dirt. The emotion he felt was unclassified in his great system of categorized realities. It was an emotion wandering untethered to any part of the apparatus he had constructed over decades. *Very curious*, he thought. *How could a thing be named if it was so decidedly detached?* Perhaps if he approached it in stillness with the contemplative focus that gained him access to the inner parts of things and ideas, his probing would force it to yield up its secret.

His collar pressed into the flesh of his neck and became moist. Constriction and hunger joined forces, drawing fuel from the stifling blather that kept everything predictable, as though this was merely death. Death. Ah, yes, yes. No doubt other funerals were scheduled for later in the day. So, there was no time to acknowledge the mystery, no room for wonder, no room for philosophy.

He turned his bull-like head toward Augusta and sniffed with a great inhalation. He sniffed again. She stared forward as he inhaled. His amygdala responded to her fragrance, alluring and yet faintly reminiscent of a wet mouse, not unpleasant, but evoking a decidedly un-platonic version of erotic desire, or perhaps an ambivalent urge to protect and console her, another frailty among the powers and principalities that were his father's airs and surrounds. He dropped his gaze to the transparent hairs on her skinny arms.

She stared forward, composed and stable, while the sweat-imbued and cloth-wrapped progeny-of-the-dead, big as a bison, and unwashed for lack of time and inclination, sniffed her. This must have required considerable concentration.

At the funeral dinner that evening Simeon watched her from a distance. She followed the old man as he moved among the gathered souls who stretched out hands of condolence, an eel swimming unharmed among the soft, caressing tentacles of stinging coral anemones, absorbing the energy of colleagues and near strangers, all gathered to eat his food, drink his wine, and gawk at his wealth. The stone mansion had often been full of the powerful, the famous, and the rich.

Simeon wished he could enjoy the theater of it all. But he could not. Neither the height of his frame, nor the breadth of his belly, nor the depth of his mind that was capable of privately pondering philosophical paradoxes while generating witty rejoinders to the desultory trivialities manufactured by the ilk populating his father's many social events, rendered Simeon, a philosopher beset with the melancholy of one who looks at history and never smiles, capable of achieving that goal so energetically pursued by the many: fitting in. Throughout the early evening while people were establishing a mood of reverie with the help of spirits, Augusta stood next to the old man, saying nothing to anyone, frantically chewing gum.

Conversations turned to the familiar world of business as men with steel-colored hair clustered and closed the circle to escape the uncanny. Augusta wandered away and sat cross-legged on an armless chair. Her knees lay flat, as though her legs were attached to her hips by rubber bands. Her back was straight, and she pressed herself firmly into the angle of the chair like a piece of folded poster board. Next to her was a small, purple, leather purse with a golden clasp, a child's purse.

Despite the density of so-called interesting people in the room rightly despised as charlatans, Simeon's attention was aimed only at his father, Augusta, and in a corner-of-the-eye way, his brother Gabriel. Gabriel ... That fierce cartoon. All angular leanness, wrapped in a suit tailored like a second skin. Uninterpretable tattoos flashed from underneath his shirtsleeves when he stretched his arms, and peeked over his collar when he cracked his neck, which he did often, as though he was always getting ready to hurt someone. The muscles of his jaws pumped like the bellows of an organ, air puffing from his nose in triple-meter as his fingers tapped texts and he ran the world as he knew it, working out his mysteries by himself. Simeon merely observed, as he had always observed from the time of his miserable endurance of preparatory school. The women in the room could not resist staring at Gabriel. He was darkly and viciously erotic. But he never paid attention to them. His glances darted around the room, but he never seemed to look at anyone in particular. He was the anti-Simeon, unplagued by the chronic observation of details that invaded Simeon's imagination when other human beings were present.

From earliest childhood, Simeon was a distant moon, hovering at the edges with a pale roundness. His own mind was a speculum, prying open the inside of things and ideas. But he was always outside the inner chamber of power that his father and brother seemed not merely to enter, but to create wherever they wandered. He had been dragged all over the world—Moscow, Berlin, London, Rome, São Paulo. The long flights became intolerable as he padded his soul with flesh through his teenage years. But he was never invited into the inner circle. The inner circle was not a place one was invited to enter. Members entered by force, by intensely negotiated rape, with cocktails and caviar. At the threshold of the chamber, he could never reach further than the couches outside his father's boardroom. Even the door to the room was intimidating with its thick-wood substantiality.

That said, what is power, really? His own mind was a recapitulation of the world of philosophical verities that his father and brother found baffling. It was beautiful, self-contained, rotating slowly, suspended within his skull, unattached to any pragmatism that might sully its purity. But when he tried to grasp the meaning of power—that inscrutable portion of invisible reality incarnated in conflict, blood sport, greed, and fate—its ontological structure eluded him, and his thoughts turned into a multisyllabic clot, often alliterative and occasionally poetic.

Augusta rose from her chair and walked toward him. The emotional pilot light deep within himself, which seemed impossible to extinguish, ignited panic in his chest. His breathing suddenly became labored. One hand held a fork, the other hand held a half-full plate. His mouth was crammed full of food, putting him at a strategic disadvantage since she was almost certain to say something.

"Excuse me." The voice was childish and squeaky. "Are you going to use those napkins?"

He looked down at the table beside his right elbow where she was pointing. He could not answer because his mouth was packed, so he grunted and nodded toward the stack of napkins. She returned to her chair and withdrew into some small world of her own. Simeon chewed his mush in a way that justified the word *mastication*, and all its resonances.

Augusta had a small amount of food on her plate, nothing but roasted duck. The strange young woman negotiated her meal in a very different way than Simeon. At first, he was uncertain about what she was doing. Then he realized she was not swallowing her food. She chewed to suck out the juice and folded the dry morsel into one of the paper napkins stacked in her lap. She placed the wad of chewed duck and napkin in her purse, and snapped shut the gold clasp. When she was done, she walked over to a wastebasket and emptied her purse into it. A new form of creature had appeared on the face of the earth, one who took only the essence and left the flesh behind, a gustatory Gnostic with gossamer tulle-tippet flesh as the only shield between her and the ever-circumambulating powers of eternal repose. His mind chattered on until suddenly she left through the same door as Gabriel, abruptly snipping the string of his plumb bob.

The rustling of coats among the guests drew him from his thoughts. The flow of bodies in the same general direction told him that the evening was near its end. His own mother had died. But he still stood in line with the other so-called mourners, wondering where Augusta and Gabriel were.

When Simeon's turn came, he reached out and shook his father's lean but crushing hand. "I'm sorry about mother." His words moved in tandem with a rising sense of his own foolishness and inadequacy.

The mechanism of the man-who-was-his-father nodded a hollow hallowed nod, as he nodded to everyone else, a secular consecration of last moments befitting to the performance of grief-at-the-death-of-one's-spouse. And then he released the hand, and his gray eyes and gray hand moved on to the next person in line like a tired preacher who long ago lost his faith, greeting his parishioners who long ago lost their faith.

Unnoticed by anyone, Simeon walked out of the great house for the last time in his life and descended to his taxicab among the limousines.

Seven years had passed since that night.

Now Augusta was coming to his home.

Well, he thought, until the work of the gods is done, the work of the gods goes on. Let her come. Let her feast her gaunt eyes upon his breadth. Was she not a child of sorts? Did not her insubstantial body outwardly manifest an equally insubstantial inward reality? Yes. Let her see him, wide as a radio telescope, receptor for signals from the world of ideas and of truth, detecting background realities that others cannot sense, reaching as far as the truth of the divine. Let her dwell for a brief time in his house filled with a solitude older than the house itself, a solitude imported from the old Russian monasteries where his great grandfather was raised. Let her visit the house where his newly dead father was raised with the discipline of a monk minus the monk's hope for God. Let her feel the house that Simeon Saint-Simone had transformed into a resting place and haven for the yearnings that embarrass an ironic age.

Yes, let her come.

2. Was der Fall ist, die Tatsache,
ist das Bestehen von Sachverhalten.

Simeon was already feeling better about himself. He picked up a handful of junk mail from the pile beside his tilt-table. Most of his mail was addressed to *Resident*, one of his anonymous peepholes on the mechanisms, gears, and powers hidden behind colorful toys and convenience items, the buy-one-get-one-frees, the complimentary gifts, the healthy-looking women and teenagers smiling, standing in their underwear, the average clean-looking men drawing together the community with their new outdoor gas grill in the valley of the dazed, surrounded by a veritable poem of plastic lauding the laudable vinyls as verities, the permanence of form at the etymological heart of plastic, the polymeric wonder made from chains of carbon forged in stars, the stuff of eggs, blood, and cattle horns, and the curse of nurdles killing birds that mistake plastic pellets for food. The force required to maintain such organization of productivity and advertisement was staggering to him.

He thumbed through the colorful junk mail until his eye settled on a gift from Providence, a brochure promising something Completely New. He almost tossed the brochure back into the pile without even running his finger along the edge to break the seal and open the triptych, the mini-altar delivered into his hand to provoke the revelation, to reveal the portal into that for which he longed, but which he was unable to state boldly and without timidity. The brochure was clearly a clue entrusted to him by the permeating aspect of the universe expressing rationality, curiosity, and the capacity to ogle. It was sent from the *Universal Church of Logophilia*. Simeon Saint-Simone had been invited to become ordained. The content of the belief system was not specified. All beliefs were encouraged in the name of Unity. For $395. Nearly nothing. The monetary equivalent of a libation offering in which the large glass of wine is consumed without guilt after letting a drop return to the earth to appease the gods. He could finally finish his doctorate, receive a license to preach, become ordained, and be granted a certificate of sainthood. Furthermore, and far more important for the nation, the required 5000-word doctoral essay would allow him to formalize his ideas for the Garden of Memory, uncovering a derelict Providence homeless among the lost souls of America. Once he received his Doctor of Immortality degree, he could advertise himself more persuasively in pamphlet form as the Reverend Doctor of The Church of the Garden of Memory, or something like that. He would be the first priest of the rediscovered Providence.

He took a carton of ice cream from the small freezer beside his tilt-table. Simeon was like a self-righting ship, the sort he had seen the Coast Guard use as they passed through the sometimes-stormy world of his window. As his world corrected by a secret mechanism hidden deep in the soul, the gears and pulleys of which he had scarcely begun to identify, he ate large, joyful bites of ice cream, savoring the chocolate morsels embedded inside the frozen cream.

Suddenly he felt a pain inside his head. Oh, the hell of eating cold things fast. He braced himself for agony. But soon a flood of grace in the form of warm blood pumped from his mysterious heart and suffused his frozen throat, and his headache subsided, leaving him with the taste of his own contingency, a reminder that he must take care even in the small things. Throats. Ice cream. What strange circumstances for a god.

He resumed his breakfast.

But he soon found himself drawn back to unwanted thoughts of Augusta. Even as a test for the feasibility of explaining the idea of the Garden of Memory to the un-initiated, the thought of her was distracting. Duck-suckers could not be expected to grasp the idea. The Master's idea. The idea of the Divine Camillo. Augusta represented the barbarism of contemporary America. She might be unable to hear the story of the whole, but she might still have ears to hear the severe and subtle significance of a list of things chosen as propaedeutic: salad shooters bought on television, hairdryers, the broken cars from a theme park ride, an old fuselage, washing machines, televisions, electric knives, electric toothbrushes, electric leg hair removers, water pics, 8 track stereos, collections of broken records without jackets, vulcanized rubber tires, broken exercise machines. Everything on the list was carefully arranged around the center-piece of his Garden, which was a wooden structure built from the description Camillo dictated to Girolamo Muzia in Milan, on seven mornings. *L'Idea del Theatro*. Within the theater was a large stove imported at great expense from Ulm.

The phone rang, startling him again. He hated that phone.

A second ring. A third. His own husky voice, weary with the slow ways of wisdom's winding path to naked unveiledness, announced his number. Then came a voice that rusts the soul—Gabriel's voice, corroding, degrading, and deceptive in masculine husk, since Gabriel had become Gabriella shortly after their mother died. "Simeon, answer the goddamn phone."

He selected a toothpick and did not answer the phone. The machine clicked off in the fuming silence of his brother Gabriella. Simeon felt a small, puerile satisfaction at his gesture of control. Dread quickly swallowed his joy. He was aware that in the night in which God hides, there is yet a darkness of extreme love that orders all and makes it accessible to the minds and hearts of a ragged, but redeemable, humanity.

The phone rang again. Things come to be that must be come to be. "Our father is dead. This means we have to meet. No one at Stump's law firm will talk to me about the estate. I know who is behind this. She will regret it. I am flying from Moscow, but I will be there soon."

"Goats of Skyros," Simeon hissed. The Stump. That stunted monstrosity who oversaw the details of their father's schemes, investments, and bankruptcies, terrorizing boards, executives, and circulating minions. His world inverted again. He took the decanter of brandy from the liquor cabinet, even though it was on the lower shelf and required considerable bending.

Few reports regarding his family ever found their way to Simeon. But he had heard that after having a vagina constructed by a specialist in France, Gabriella had become fiercer and more aggressive than ever in her businesses. She was full of hunger for wealth and power and conflict. But she was oblivious to the stasis of milieu. She ignored the barnacles of history accruing to the hull of civilization's ship in the wake of her actions.

"Carpets and cushions of Carthage!" He needed a more persuasive and substantial outburst that would better fit the interruptions that Providence was inexplicably introducing into his life. Then the phrase occurred to him: "Angor animi!"

He whispered the phrase several times over the lip of the graceful snifter filled with amber essence. The ancient words that once brought him a universe of comfort thinned as he thought of the fumes that were pouring forth from Gabriella's jet thirty thousand feet above the human-sized world.

Suddenly he sneezed and brandy went into his nose. His nose was cavernous, Socratic, and sensitive to pain. His eyes began to water, and he was emptied of any sense of well-being. He wiped his puffy, fat eyelids, wet with tears. How could dignity be maintained in a body? So much malfunction, so much dissolution in the material world, such sadness, such a cloud upon the brow resisting remedies of baths and the consumption of cabbages. Function and malfunction.

And yet, he loved the look of old cars in the field, weeds growing through the grill. He loved the look of telephone poles leaning and covered in kudzu. Could anyone keep track of the maintenance the poles needed? It all had to rot eventually. The crust of technology had to grow thin and fragile until the lava of philosophy burned its way to the surface, consuming the frivolous decadence of contemporary invention that no longer grew from the wholesome and poetic Edisonian inventory for devising devices—screws, needles, cords, wire, hair of human, hair of horse, hair of hog, hair of hare, camel, goat, and minx, silk, cocoon, hoofs, teeth, deer horns, tortoise shells, amber, cork, ore, and feathers from the ostrich and the peacock's tail—decadent invention calculated to yield devices that lure the masses toward the traps of webs and nets, where the bodies of strangers and the agonies of the anonymous, caught on surveillance cameras, could be broadcast and cast broadly, with no sign at the gate, *Abandon Hope All Ye Who Enter Here*, but rather mere appeal to desire, "Do you wish to enter this site?" requiring only an electronic *yes*, an *e-yes* to bring abomination to the eyes . . .

He was growing weary of his bardic brain. And he had not yet even escaped the morning. He needed Jerome's presence both to hear his trivialities and to disrupt the flow of words. He picked up his walkie-talkie. "Jerome. Jerome. Are you awake? We have work to do."

Jerome did not answer. Simeon looked down at the ill and ancient lion reclining on the ground beside the wooden replica of Camillo's Theater of Memory where Jerome no doubt slept, lolling on the roll-up mattress he kept on the stage, warmed by the great stove from Ulm.

"Cyprian juice of convolvulus." The voice in Simeon's brain was in quite a mood. He wiped away the mucousy brandy from his upper lip. There was only silence skimming the background of the sound of the sibilant sea. The wind clapped, using a loose shutter to show up in the aural world.

Convolvulus ... the word inflicted on his mind by the voice—convolvulus, convolvuli, evolving to con-vulva, to be with vulva, that vestibule to mystery, to . . .

"You called?" Jerome's weary voice inflected halfway between the interrogative and the observational.

Simeon lifted his walkie-talkie. "Yes, Jerome. I require your service. Come immediately."

Jerome sighed. Twice. Simeon knew that he deliberately held down the talk-button while he released his second psalmic sigh, as if to say, *how long, oh Lord, how long?*

"I'll come up after my tea."

Simeon found it difficult to maintain the proper formality with Jerome. Jerome was his only employee. He was prone to mention looking for another job (as though a worn-out old Cuban could get a job with the wage Simeon paid and the free space within the world's only replica of Camillo's Theater of Memory). Nonetheless, Simeon would wait until Jerome had finished his tea. What else could he do?

He looked around at the philosophical storehouse in which he lived, full of resources to meet nearly any emergency of meaning, interpretation, utterance, or therapeutic condescension. His house was full of the marks of wisdom and wastefulness, but it felt suddenly vacuous, with the switch of perspective old LW explored with his duck-rabbit.

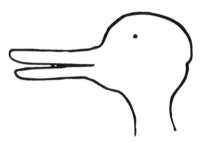

One moment his Garden of Memory, with the artifacts of barbarism embedded within its boundaries, seemed to reveal an as-yet unspeakable truth about the world. The next moment, as lightning in the dark briefly illuminates the wolves among the trees, contingency bared its teeth, and his collection looked more than ever like junk.

"Nectars of Lesbos," he grumbled. Time slowed

down. He anxiously awaited the full awakening of Jerome who, like David playing the harp for Saul, would use his droll commentary on the day's events to distract Simeon from the voice that always chattered in the background of his mind, a voice trapped behind some fragile web of neurons, clawing, threatening at any moment, with just one too many mental stresses, to poke the crazed nail through the tender mesh and take up full residence in the luxurious space of his enormous brain.

That voice he knew. It was the voice of his brother, *the mysterious other*. Not Gabriella ... Simeon was supposed to be a twin. But early in gestation, the other twin was diminished to naught after a small amount of bleeding. His mother thought she had lost both. But Simeon remained behind, curled up like an apostrophe designating the possessive to the event of his brother's demise. Simeon had a theory: he had resorbed his twin, but the twin was only half-related to him. Simeon's true father, he believed with subtle biological speculation, was a stranger. This theory explained so much. The muttering, his own great bulk, the fact that even in years of apparent solitude, he rarely felt lonely, the fact that he was continuously anxious in exactly the way a man carrying another person inside his brain might expect. The factual basis for anxiety about carrying a partial stranger in his brain required only a uterine fraternity within a mother resulting from the wondrous eroto-emergent sloppiness of nature, that heteropaternal superfecundation in which a flirty fisher can receive the seed of two men in a time of exuberant ovulation, with two ova floating down the fallopian brook, egg-the-first absorbing the message-in-a-bottle from man-one, and egg-the-second given a reprieve from obliteration by the surprise arrival of back up troops from man-two. His own mother, of course, was probably not a flirty fisher. But the biological possibility left him gobsmacked.

"Bah," he finally called out to the emptiness of the room. He reached for the flattened cigarette package on his table.

How he wished he could have only the small, manageable Augusta rather than the suffocating presence of his brother Gabriella. When he last heard about Gabriella she had invested a large part of her fortune in an American train company expanding around the world, crushing its way through various small pockets of culture and history.

Perhaps she would come and quickly consolidate her grasp on their father's estate, and then leave forever. Simeon required very little to support his philosophical research: cigarettes, ouzo, TV dinners, freedom from traditional labor, and a reasonable fund for the selective purchase of America's discarded waste to place in the Garden of Memory, which stood as a monument against the lazy dumping practices that lead to liquid leachate, litter flying on the winds, and the foul nourishment of unclean beasts and ravenous vermin. More than any of this, however, he needed his privacy, for which he would gladly exchange any fortune left to him.

He pulled out a new package of cigarettes from the drawer of his table, which Jerome kept full as a small form of security plugging one leak in the dam of dread. He lit the cigarette and relaxed his body, big as a walrus, thinking multifarious thoughts about the world, and feeling his member go through cycles of expansion and retreat as his attention variably turned to and from the young women on the beach below. He tried again to provoke the as-yet unnamed twin to converse, rather than chattering in monologue. But for the moment all the wretch would do is to repeat his name, "Simeon, Simeon, Simeon," forcing him to an early start on the strenuous work of producing notecards to exorcise the babel and fill the chests in the Theater of Memory.

Back to Augusta. Who was this so-called Augusta? What was on her vitae? Data, information, insight, strategy—this is what he needed. So, Augusta. Fact: she lived for seven years with Peter Saint-Simone. Fact: she said her life work would soon begin. Fact: she was planning a funeral dinner.

And why would she worry that someone might be killed? Had she changed in the years of castle-dwelling? Simeon had always hated his father's massive stone house, austere throughout, except for the public rooms where the old man indulged the cravings of his guests. No warm lamps for reading, no rich colors, no rugs, no wood in the fireplace, no music boxes, no world globes provoking wanderlust and longing. There were only rooms occupied by the abstractions of height, length, and breadth, places where mourning was swallowed by silence, with one strange exception: on the high domed ceiling of the library, Peter Saint-Simone had commissioned a painting with shadows thrown by churning clouds, a blue heaven, and Dante's Beatrice peering down from the edge of the painting, surrounded by the calmness of angels living on ideas and light. She looked like she cared nothing for the pain in the world below, not from cruelty so much as from an untouched vision of God's goodness, unchanging, whatever suffering might occur beneath the beatific vision. Beautiful Beatrice, married but never marred, Bice di Folco Portinari, married to Simone de Bardi instead of Dante, the distant one for whom she became the glorious lady of mind, and soul, and body. That lucky poet was blessed with a dead muse. Simeon the Bard had only the loon of his twin reclining on a crescent in his cortex. Oh, for a Beatrice.

His father devoured knowledge as ammunition for his never-ending battles. In the empty cave of his great, unadorned library, the books hung on the walls like bats, with wings tucked around the alien bristles of grumbling bellies. His father read while sitting on a wooden chair, a man gray and formal, never lighting the fire in the fireplace, refusing to allow even the library's hearth to glow like a tiny heart in the middle of a dark beast. As a child, Simeon would wind around the four-level walkways held in the air by wires and bolts, like the rigging of a theater stage for the entrance of heavenly creatures, or ghouls of the sky. But with his father there, the library was a silent tomb, and reading risked the violence of breaking the spines of books, or introducing other vicissitudes and marks of mutability.

The library was a cave of thresholds where Simeon encountered many firsts, and learned to govern the emptiness of the upper tiers near the calm blue of Beatrice's bliss, while he stared down into the pit where his solitary father drew strength from planning the ruin of many, occasionally hurling some anthologized barb at Simeon's mind, asking him to comment.

But back to facts. Fact: somewhere, if Augusta told the truth, the body of Peter Saint-Simone must be lying on a mortician's slab, bloated, purple, sour.

The time had come to face and conquer the blank pages in the book of memory, waking to a pining grief weeping at death, villainous and cruel, finding no solace in false simulacra and skilled ballads about throbbing pulses responding to her face endowed and endured, the sum of bewilderment, as portents and omens of a rotting countenance incline the mind toward sweet and unavoidable death, the vernacular of the wagging tongue hissing in violent sighs against mortal pallor and orbs of longing, the need for that which is beyond the widest of celestial spheres. If one thought of her in that way, Augusta represented a credible course of life, curriculum vitae, CV.

Simeon opened his eyes. He had briefly dozed. He lit a cigarette. In four long draws it was gone. He breathed out the last puff of smoke, repositioning himself upright on his tilt-table as the day began again. Suddenly he remembered that Augusta was to come later in the day. His fare was the common viand of dread with which he was overstuffed, as his mind turned toward the reality that his brother, the mincing charlatan who would sing hymns of hell, was also flying in to torment him. He wanted to drink great quantities of wine, a mortal's cure for sorrow. But his oenologizing mind held steady in the winds of rapid-onset thought, and he knew that he should only drink enough to free the ideas lurking in the dark crypts of his brain. He had to distinguish syllables with his tongue, and avoid the slosh of slurred words that would make his brother despise him even more than the heft of his flesh already did. He would need a proper morning nap to prepare. But that would require going to his bedroom.

He decided against this move, though the prospect of an extra nap in his enormous bed usually felt like a little gift from Providence. He enjoyed sitting in his bed looking out the window at the backside of his Garden of Memory, which surrounded his sea-side Victorian mansion. From that window, he could survey the homes of those without wisdom, his complaining neighbors to whom the Garden seemed to be just a junkyard.

The tenaciousness of their misperception was baffling. More than once he had printed brochures outlining the purposes and merits of the Garden of Memory, using terms a commoner could understand. Several times he had sent Jerome around the neighborhood with the brochures to stockpile good will, against the inevitable day when some new acquisition would challenge his neighbors' diminutive capacity for insight, an acquisition such as the elderly lion he had purchased a week prior from a family-run zoo that was bankrupt—a lovely creature that slept day and night inside a large, concrete section of a city sewer pipe Simeon had bought, coming out only to nibble on the tub of food Jerome had to cut up and soften since the lion was missing most of his teeth. But all of this was vanity under the sun, for their minds were unmovable.

If the Garden was to survive his death there would have to be some longer account of the underlying idea. Death, his deadline, was not a happy thought. He would never claim the Garden was finished. Instead, his book would be a set of rules for growing the Garden, not outwardly as with crass material expressions of greed evolving into sprawl, but inwardly, intensifying in meaning, growing with the rhythm and pace of some ecclesial algorithm, with feast days and seasons of ordinary time.

The key to the Garden was, to the untrained eye, deceptively simple. Simeon had acquired an old card catalogue thrown out by the local library when they computerized their book retrieval system. Jerome secured this to a wagon so he could pull it around the Garden.

The path through the maze of the Garden was smooth and carefully tended by Jerome. In the cart, Simeon stored wisdom and clues on index cards. On some of the cards he scribbled quotes from the philosophers who had written since the time of Descartes' great Joke, with contrasting references to philosophers before Descartes, each point symbolized by a different constellation of numbered objects in the Garden arranged in clusters. He had cross-referenced snippets from political speeches, newspapers, and advertisements. He had pages from the TV guide, partial transcripts of some of the 700 Club's Christian broadcasts, and guest lists from the Jerry Springer show that included biographical details of each person.

The system had become enormously complex over the years, and in places, he would admit, it was unwieldy and inadequately organized. This is why he contemplated a single book, a prolegomenon to the entire enterprise. So far, he had only worked on the title. He liked the title *Tractatus Gastronomicus*, because it fit his philosophical technique of consuming and incorporating the world into his very flesh in order to most fully grasp the inner truth of things by becoming one substance with them. The title also allowed him to contrast his own approach to "everything that is the case" with that of good old LW, who tended toward the abstemious. He liked the simplicity of the alternate title, *Idea*, a title that had an attractive resonance with the book of the Master, Camillo. But there was a new title floating in the lower regions of his mind. It might be the best title of all for a book that would finally give a full account of the origin of wars, harlotry, murders, and unjust pillaging, as well as the variety of victuals the human mouth desires to suck, chomp, and savor in order to stave off untuneful wails of hunger that make the complexion grow pale—the bean, the lupine, the turnip, the vetch, the deep-fried insouciant cicada, the chick-pea, the pontic nut, the fig—poems of flavors and cravings of the loins that urgently demanded a treatise: *The Phenomenology of Desire*.

In contrast to the thrill of thinking about jotting down notes for an outline of such a magnificent book as *The PoD*, the morning was dulled by the actual tasks his day would hold—the distractions of Augusta and Gabriella. He felt that he might never find the energy to write the actual book, nay, even to decide upon a title, despite the presence of Jerome, the librarian of the infinite. The dull mental fog would eventually dissipate, of course, but his inability to systematically scribble the volumes of his inner world would linger in the wings of his soul, taunting him. And without the book, his life-work would spiral away like so much shredded confetti in a wind after a military parade, leaving no trace of the organizing reason and meaning for the event, the event of Simeon Saint-Simone. Then comes the street sweeper. Then to the garbage dump. And then it is all over.

He scratched an itching bump on his buttocks. He had once heard that melanoma itches. He pulled out two mirrors he kept in the drawer next to the tilt-table for the purpose of visualizing portions of his body hidden by his substance, and he could see that the bump was flesh-colored, not dark. But he had also heard that melanoma can be flesh-colored.

He lit another cigarette. He had become strangely convinced through some process of reasoning, the details of which he could not recall exactly, that coffee and cigarettes prevented stomach ulcers in him alone, given his singular physiology.

What dullness. Only a couple of hours earlier he had still been ignorant of the approaching horror, and he had lolled happily in his bed beside the large bedroom window from which he watched his next-door neighbor roll his garbage bin down the sidewalk, holding it away from his expensive suit. Anytime the man looked over at the Garden of Memory, his face formed itself into a glowering droop.

That man, Simeon inwardly seethed. So efficient. Such an early riser, jogging at 5:00 in the morning, resisting the inevitable death of his aging body. Good God, Simeon thought. Far better to pursue philosophy and ready himself for death than to try delaying it. And when the neighbor would pull out of his driveway in his Jaguar convertible with the top down, Simeon's nimble imagination would propel itself to the office building where coworkers would see his thick gray and wind-blown hair, and perhaps mistake him for a slightly wild spirit instead of who he truly was, the aging man afraid of death.

The position of his bed beside the window also allowed him to start each day by looking toward the stone head of his great grandfather's statue rising up from the middle of the town, visible over the palm trees. Good old great grandfather, he thought, as he thought every morning. The sculptor had intended a resolute stare out to sea, fearless, looking toward the old world with satisfaction from the new. But by some perversity wrought by the god of lapidaries, the stone eyes angled slightly downward, gazing instead upon Simeon's window where every morning he stood naked, smoking, feeling judgment upon his life by his hungry and productive family. This was a thought that plunged to the tenderest parts of his dark heart.

Simeon wept.

As quickly as the wave of tears came, they stopped, and he looked out over his large red cheeks, and allowed himself to be briefly cheered by the pudendal suggestiveness of the modern bikini. With this comforting image in mind he closed his eyes again, just for a short nap.

He awoke to the feel of a pleasant breeze from the sea blowing over the dunes of his mostly-naked body. The smell of food drifted from some pleasant source. His mind wandered the bridge from dreams to middling thoughts of moon-women and cultivated mallow with comb-like resemblance to placenta, thence to the other side of waking where the cold saltwater of a voice from behind splashed on him.

"I will wait until you are dressed."

He glanced at the mirror on the wall and saw Augusta standing in his home, pondering his ponderous presence. Simeon, naked on the tilt-table, glared at her in the mirror as though by force of will he could make her wither to a sapless remnant blowable by winds.

She wore an expensive black suit made of the same kind of cloth his father ordered for his own suits. He looked at the subtle lined pattern of the suit, and suddenly he knew that it *was* one of his father's own suits, cut down by two thirds to fit her austere frailty. The fine tailoring did not hide the gaunt reality of her bony arms and shoulders from which rose the pale twig of her neck, white as a peeled birch limb. Her hair was cut to look like a waif, but rather than the greenish tinge that lingered in his memory, it was dyed metallic gray. She was as fleshless as his saints.

"You …" he tried to say, so filled with the sense of unutterable invasion that he made no effort to cover any part of the naked cascade of his body. Decades of solitude had left him unprepared for this.

She walked to the side of his tilt-table and surveyed his circumference with a calculated leisure. Her expression did not change. She was betrayed by no gesture or word. But he still felt disgust for his expansive body radiating from her abstemious and falsely-aged presence. "I have made breakfast for you Simeon."

He wiped the crust from the corners of his eyes. A question rose to his dry lips. With a voice rough from sinus drainage and his morning cigarettes he asked, "How long have you been here?"

She pulled out the platinum Patek Philippe pocket watch that Simeon recognized as the old man's. She opened it. "Forty-seven minutes." She clicked the watch shut with the same crisp gesture his father had always used.

His morning nausea swelled with this click of the watch, and his eyes began to tear with frustration, a physiological response he despised, but one he could not control any more than he controlled the migrating myoelectric oracle of borborygmous babbling from his belly in the public library reading room. This snapping of the watch was a gratuitous offense.

"Go get dressed, Simeon. You will enjoy the breakfast I have made for you."

His groggy cortex mapped the consequences of appearing passively obedient. He pictured himself shuffling toward his bedroom, sliding his feet so that his slippers did not fall off, making no effort to cover his pale and sagging buttocks. He gathered the resolve to speak, and forthwith his mouth did utter, "Blue blazes, you shiny fig pecker." He paused to assess his chances of saying something more forceful, something that would sting her and give him the advantage. "Consort not with the octopus, strumpet, and relieve me of your radishy presence." He kneaded his jowls and tried to gather in the magnitude of his new misfortune, as he seemed unable to say anything fitting to the occasion.

Just then Jerome the Blessed spoke over the walkie-talkie. "I guess you'll want to go on rounds today? I reattached the couch to the floor of the pickup. I used very big bolts this time. They were on sale."

Simeon felt the relief of weary warriors who hear the sounds of the hooves of fresh cavalry coming over hills from behind. He picked up his walkie-talkie. "No Jerome. We will not be scouting for additions to the Garden, nor shopping for honey-cakes and gruel. Today we have a visitor. Come up, I say, come up."

Over the walkie-talkie came a great sigh.

Augusta drummed her fingernails against the metal of the pocket watch, making a sound like a toothy rat scurrying across the floor. "Get dressed. You are ridiculous lying there naked. We have too much to talk about and very little time. Your life is about to change." With that she went to the kitchen, leaving him to wonder about which parts of the house she had invaded during his morning nap.

There were, he inwardly acknowledged, yet more facts to be dealt with.

He smoked several cigarettes, lighting one off the other, waiting for some resolution to form. Finally, with one hand full of the unshaven flesh of his face, he decided that he would meet her with the collected force of his years of constructing a cosmos. She was standing in an oasis of which he was ruler, king. The philosopher-king might be the height of irony in the mundane world, but this was not the mundane world. This was the domain of Simeon Saint-Simone, watched over by gods veiled in the saffron robes of sunrise and sunset. Here at least he was not without some power.

A gathering headache began to occupy his massive calvarium, no doubt an aneurysm or a brain tumor gesturing to him, bidding him goodbye with a sneer. He pressed on the sides of his head.

Jerome's voice bellowed, with a strangely subdued bellow, over the walkie-talkie. "Agathon." *Agathon*, absurdly, was the only name Jerome would use to address Simeon directly—Simeon's rules precluded the use of his first name by an employee, and Jerome was unwilling to call him *Mr. Saint-Simone,* in part because it was awkward, given Jerome's comparable intellect, recognized by both men, and in part because Jerome knew it would remind Simeon that he was a *Mr.* and not a *Dr.,* and that was a sore spot. Jerome had picked the name himself, and he refused to tell Simeon the significance of it.

At the same time Jerome calmly grated on Simeon's consciousness over the walkie-talkie, the inner voice appeared within his throbbing head, speaking from the same place as the headache, "Simeon. Simeon. Simeon."

He closed his eyes and covered them with the thick flesh of his hands. He tried to control the throb of his headache as he endured the echo in the architecture of his mind, grasping for the eternal aspect of all things, his mind itself a theater, a place in which a spectacle unfolds according to the order of the creation of the world, turning the inward scholar into a spectator of all that is manifest, the original and essential ingredients, with time past arranged in space upon the walls of the temple between his temples, the order of the whole resting on Solomon's Seven Pillars of Wisdom, which in turn hold up the Moon, Mercury, Venus, Mars, Jupiter, and Saturn, the upper levels flowing thence and organizing all that is given to man to do, Banquet and Cave where creation began, Gorgons and Pasiphae where the wondrous reality of the inward man is shown in relation to the cosmos, Sandals of Mercury and Prometheus showing forth the acts of mankind erupting through arts, and engines, and the work of conducting the world. Residing as the Theater's custodian, with the clarity of beatitude, was the *ignis fatuus* of his twin dressed in red ornate robes with coins and beads sewn to the hems, nimbly skirting the convolution of grooves and fissures that constituted the dwelling place of his mind. His provocative twin named himself Giulio, which was unfair because one ought not to name oneself. His gaze was benevolently condescending, as he tucked his vague chin into the fat of his phosphoric neck, gently mocking Simeon in retaliation for being resorbed in the womb, stopping in the midst of the pain in Simeon's head to sniff the air, scooping toward his nostrils the fragrance of the breakfast Augusta was cooking, and pronouncing rather late, "I call the day into session."

Simeon replied under the strain of pained thought, "I shall hire an exorcist if you chatter on," though the smell of cooking food did ease the ache considerably.

3. Das logische Bild der Tatsachen ist der Gedanke.

Simeon looked forward to assessing what Augusta meant by *breakfast*, but he was also occupied with weighing the value of Pascal's regard for flies as being so mighty that they win battles, paralyze our minds, eat up our bodies. Only in the Idea would he find refuge from frailty. He was to complete the work of the Divine Camillo. That he knew. Less obvious was the methodology that would best fit the work ordained by Providence.

In the opening of *L'Idea del theatro*, Camillo observed that the most ancient and wisest of writers placed the secrets of God under obscure veils in order to keep them from everyone except those with the will to suffer the rays of divinity. Philosophers were right to cover their most profound discoveries with fables in order to keep them from being profaned. The actual instantiation of his intuited purpose for using Camillo's Theater as a guide for the construction of his own work was not clear. Not crystal. Not yet.

Camillo described his theater as having seven steps divided by seven gangways representing the seven planets. A visitor to the theater stood as spectator looking out over the seven measures of the world, lolling where the stage usually was, staring out toward the auditorium where images were lodged on the seven rising grades. These were the memory places. The whole system rested upon the seven pillars of Solomon's House of Wisdom, the seven measures of the fabric of the celestial and inferior worlds, containing the Ideas of all things in both worlds. Camillo chose his seven planets, but he skipped the Earth. Some might be confused by that, but not Simeon. Providence had reserved the Earth for him, the last remaining human (aside from Jerome the Cuban, possibly) who could grasp the first principle of the theater: humanity is divine, able to remember the universe by looking down upon it from above, from First Causes, as might a god. The looming demise of humanity was caused by forgetting the principle. What else could it possibly be? And so, obviously, the hope for humanity was the recollection of the principle, the rebirth of this eternal truth, with Simeon as midwife.

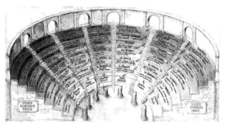

His most recent method was to incarnate ideas using garbage, the category of discarded form. As Camillo's structure carried the mind through seven rising grades that progressed from nature to artifact, Simeon's structure would complete the system by carrying the mind from artifact to garbage. Providence regularly delivered just the right pieces of garbage for the day's work. He might wake up and start by thinking how his distant feet seemed strange to him, cold and earthy with their thick, long toenails. And then, in a moment, *mirabile dictu*, the morning newspaper would reveal to him an advertisement selling a box of outdated prostheses found in the attic of the house of an orthopod's old widow. Lost limbs fascinated him.

Or he might be riding along in the bed of the pick-up truck fitted with the love seat anchored to the floor, and the extra-large seat belt, installed by the ever-worried Jerome, screwed into the frame to keep him secure, when suddenly the clouds would part, and the sun would illuminate a pile of belongings on the side of the road that some forsaken lover had finally pitched in despair, and he would tap on the window to tell Jerome to pull over. Truth rose up from the world. No venture into the chaos of the dark inkpot was needed. Just eyes, ears, and a nose able to remain stalwart in the face of all bodily smells.

When Simeon would tap on the truck window Jerome would pull the truck alongside the curb, smoke pouring from the tailpipe rattling bass. They would wait a few minutes to make sure that no angry second thoughts brought the injured out onto the porch. Then Jerome would begin loading the discarded items according to the wishes of the Philosopher, feeling for the ragged edges of reality, the artifacts of loss and emotion, the ache of erotic imagination and betrayal, and the way the unutterable ache is expressed in throwing out the traces and the veils manifesting the invisible desired one: favorite old LPs once listened to in bliss, boxes of flannel shirts with the smell of work into which the nose might burrow for comfort, the sunglasses that made the face so mysteriously handsome in the distance, the shaving utensils, colognes, mouth washes, eye drops, nose drops, ear drops, and talcum powders, all once actively used to care for the beloved body, the travel magazines that should have been the first hint that he was leaving, and even the old key collection which he compulsively grew in a shoe box without knowing what any of the keys opened, a divinely conferred metaphor for a culture without memory—clues available only in a society prone to discarding, a kind of public nakedness of soul.

But obviously, he could not be entirely catholic in his acceptance of rubbish, just as Camillo could not accept all statements of wisdom about the world. A list of everything adds nothing to our understanding of the world. Everything is merely everything. Something more than everything was needed. The world is the world. The Theater of Memory—and, to complete the work, its humble descendant, the Garden—had to represent the whole in much less space. Memory is not *all that is the case*. It is an organizing principle. That is where the divine element can be found by the elect.

Jerome would finish loading up the chosen items, exaggerating his desultory lankiness to suggest, without words, that his true gifts were severely underemployed, slowing his movements until Simeon felt light-headed from the old pickup's fumes wafting up to his love seat. Eventually they would go home to sort through, and interpret, the booty. Simeon had purchased the pair of walkie-talkies so that he could direct the labor of Jerome. Sitting high upon his tilt-table, all the world at his feet, he pressed in on the discovery that was right at his fingertips. He was almost there.

He often wished for the simple life of Jerome: Jerome, a man conditioned to make do with what he had, formed virtuously by his hidden and mysterious struggles in Cuba, where old technology had to be lovingly maintained, demanding ingenuity, a mechanical manifestation of a good Hegelian infinity, directed toward internal coherence and intensification rather than stretching forever in the endless direction of *more* and *new* and *improved*. Jerome's placid face rarely changed as his mind tended toward the inscape of his small world, making his modest wage, living in the wooden replica of Camillo's Theater, never questioning the arrangement of the Garden of Memory, or its purpose, or the necessity of such additions as the ancient and nearly toothless lion. Despite his many indecipherable sighs, Jerome did not seem to desire any more trappings of security, even though gray appeared in his beard and hair. No one ever visited him. Simeon envied the simplicity of the pragmatic scholar, innocent of the endless weight of irony, the burden of prophesying to the modern slaves of forgetfulness, the agony of being a seer who appeared to be piddling among relics while the whole world rotted from the inside. But at the end of day, Jerome seemed to think inscrutable thoughts while sitting on top of the Theater in the waning light, staring out to sea, refusing to reveal his mind, though Simeon suspected that beneath his doleful demeanor, the inward being of Jerome the Cuban strived to grasp the muting of the immutable, the effing of the ineffable.

Augusta's cooking was quickly winning olfactory points. The simple pleasure of smell reminded him how naturally the world tends toward normality. His room was his room, his mind was silent, his headache was dissipating. May the gods be praised.

He reached for a cigarette.

Down below the garbage men drove up in their truck, deftly navigating the space between the wall of Simeon's Garden and the artificially perfect landscaping of his neighbor's property. The driver was not as big as Simeon, but he was close. He turned the large steering wheel to maneuver the truck while his much thinner colleague frenetically jumped on and off, attaching garbage bins to the lift on back, carrying away the waste. What useful and unmetaphysical beauty the whole procedure was, carrying away the refuse of fallen gods, leaving only the residuum of insight into immortality, the infallible argument that if a soul is known by a timeless God, it is known for eternity, implying immortality for the simple reason that a soul cannot be known without being real, a conclusion made problematic only because of the corollary consequence that the argument seemed also to make beetles immortal, and miscarried porpoises, and every bacteria flushed down the toilet despite being known to the mind of an omniscient deity. And yet, why not? Why not a profligate immortality? Maybe that was the lesson of garbage, garbage as the modern *analogia entis*.

His neighbor's garbage fell into the truck, an inassimilable abundance collected before Simeon's eyes. The bin returned to the sidewalk and a great metal shield lowered and scooped the abundance into the cavern of the truck's hold.

Augusta opened the kitchen door and said, "Breakfast is ready. Why are you still naked?"

Simeon should have been a garbage truck driver. What meditations he could have had, driving around the city, cleaning up things. But that was never to be. No. His lot was Augusta, distracting him from his contemplative labors. Of course, she would not go away if he merely ignored her. He breathed in a deep, gratuitously free breath, and he tried to overcome the sense of being a jester in his own court. "Why are you in my house?"

"I told you I was coming. You didn't say no."

He allowed his face to rock forward slightly in deference to genuine disbelief. If she was willing to say such a thing, contradicting the manifest reality of the situation, she was no doubt willing to say anything. Unreason, his old enemy, was back in town.

"I did not invite you."

"You didn't say no," she repeated. Her slender neck momentarily distracted him. A large man might bite through it completely with a few enthusiastic chomps.

"But I didn't even pick up the phone."

"You could have, if you really didn't want me to come."

Petty evil tapped for chinks in the armor of his world, slithering into the very sanctuary of philosophical reverence. "Are those my father's clothes?"

"They are." She spread her arms to display the finely re-tailored suit.

"And the pocket watch?"

She patted the pocket in which it was tucked.

Bloody blue blazes. Before the old man's temperature had equilibrated with the earth, she was plucking goodies from his dresser drawer and shrinking his suits to fit her diminutive frame. Well, let her have it. Let her have anything and everything that might expedite her departure. No doubt that is the only reason she had come.

"I made you breakfast. Do you want to eat it in here?"

He usually sat on a piano bench by his card table to eat his TV dinners, but he would not move for her. He would defy her.

He refused to answer. He rested his face in his hands and gently stroked the whiskers on his neck with his thumbs, thinking, thinking, nearly regretting the way the smell of the food blunted his seething anger, his anxiety, his gloomy mire.

"Fine," she said. "I will bring it in here." She went to the kitchen and made clinking noises with dishes.

He turned on his television. To ignore her properly would require an alternate focus that compelled. Breakfast was probably her version of frankincense, gold, and myrrh, gifts to lure him into her plans before telling him what they were. He was acquainted with the strategies common to the species.

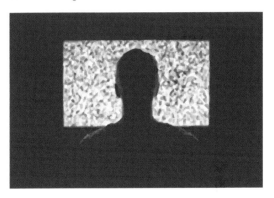

Watching television was too passive for Simeon's great brain. Simeon observed television, and monitored the world from this observatory. With the click of a button the great eye rotated to various segments of the battleground. First came a shopping advisory, a novel class of news never before thought of in the history of the world. The well-groomed young man reported on recent developments in the case of someone who put rat poison into jars of baby food.

After a cursory introduction to whet the appetite, followed by a heart-felt report detailing the various fears and anxieties of suburban parents, they broke to a commercial for a special salad chopper, fitting the tragedy into the time between commercials, constrained by the need to move on to lighter-hearted segments, balancing the emotions of the more passive watchers-of-television who knew not what they did. He scribbled down the number. He never ate salad, but he had never seen a chopper of this exact sort. And the list of freebies added on as a reward for ordering grew, which made the expenditure less and less painful to the average consumer. Simeon was not the average consumer.

The newscaster returned. He moved on to jokes about mistaken weather predictions before the camera swung to the meteorologist. Had everyone forgotten the child who became so sick from the rat poison in his baby food that a well-meaning mother gave trying to nourish her progeny?

He needed the secret mechanism to set his own world aright. That, and the actual breakfast. The longer he smelled breakfast, the more he desired to taste it, to devour and digest it, abstracting form from matter, sending the one from his stomach up to the mind and the other down to the sewer, his reflections slipping quickly toward the jejune in their leap from desire to the jejunal alchemy that transforms the dead into nutrient, memory, and poop. He changed the channel to cartoons and lit a cigarette to take the edge off his impatience. He farted loudly. He was suddenly embarrassed for the first time in decades. The feeling took him by surprise, especially after enduring the exposure of his naked flesh to the gaze of the diminutive Augusta.

He listened closely. The bustling in the kitchen continued. Maybe she did not hear him. He sniffed. Not bad, quickly dissipating, then conquered completely by the smell of breakfast. Once vulnerability to embarrassment faded, he acknowledged that one should have reminders of shame, occasionally, to add depth to the soul.

He switched channels and listened to a thick man discuss the fact that the index of consumer sentiment was down. Here too was new a category of human assessment, a measure of value unthought of in the history of philosophical anthropology. The index of consumer sentiment. He had only to absorb the riches forged in the furnace of economic ambition and to record the detritus of barbarian ambitions in his Garden, with reference cards as guide. He did not have to strain to find ways of expanding philosophy's vocabulary. All this was done for him on the news.

Augusta appeared with an empty plate, a knife, and a fork. He tried not to show interest, but he felt like a dog that knows the master is about to fill his bowl.

Simeon never used plates since he subsisted on hundreds of frozen dinners contained in convenient, disposable packages heatable in the oven or the microwave. He kept the disposable containers, smashing them through the week in a trash compactor he bought for this purpose. He saved the bags of compressed trays as a reminder of the meals he had eaten, a reminder in the sense of number and abstraction, though the meals themselves were processed food, and thus singularly unmemorable. His gustatory questions involved testing the extent to which all bodily function could be made commercial, generic, asking what, if anything, is not transformable into the language of consuming, consorting with the purveyors of mass-produced blandness in the spirit of the prophet Hosea who took for himself a wife of whoredom named, of all things, Gomer. In the years of bearing witness, he had collected nearly twenty thousand of these trays, pressed and stacked in a corner of the yard, an ethylenic polylith.

At last she brought in the food on a rolling cart. He

breathed in, preparing himself for restraint. She set out six small ham brioches. They were like enough unto one other, but each had its own attraction, voluptuous loaves stirring his heart. Her Spanish egg casserole was a light-yellow fluff of egg in a matrix of cheese, thrust through with the bold reds, greens, and onion-whites of the southern lands. He inwardly rejoiced.

He began to eat without a word, all philosophical and popular distractions fading to reverent silence as something long-forgotten seemed to stir, something nurtured in the dark eddies of his heart, awaiting a moment such as this to rise.

She set before him a simple bowl of cut fruit—kiwi, mango, cantaloupe, honeydew. This did not leap toward him with the insistence of the brioche and the casserole until she augmented it with a symmetrically placed bowl of crème fraiche. Finally, she placed before him a stack of 10 biscuits with butter and jam to the side.

Only then did she sit. He rotated his heavy head and turned his eyes toward her. With a lift of his eyebrows he indicated the question whether or not she would join him, or perhaps whether or not she would leave so that he might eat without the sense of being watched, and so, being judged as a gaping cuckoo with legs fatter than a ripe seedless watermelon.

"I have eaten," she said, interpreting the signs upon his face. "This is for you."

He grunted past the chasmal resonance of his nasal breathing, and the grind and slosh of mastication.

She. The thought arose from within the stasis of unsated appetite, an involuntary consciousness of the odd fact that he had never had a female inside his house. *Girl,* the world swirled. Something shifted from center, and to halt the tumble he reached for a biscuit and put it whole into his mouth, so that his mouth was filled with delicate crumbling substance as he bit through the bread's flesh. Up and down he chewed, feeling a long-forgotten contentment at the fluffy flour tasting faintly of butter, with hints of sweetness and of herbs strangely redolent of blite-berry and sprigs of chervil. But these raptures made him feel silly before the gaunt eyes of the creator who weighed less than one of his legs.

Augusta turned off the cartoons, a gesture that broke his concentration, and she said, "I want to tell you something."

He stopped chewing and glared at her forehead until she turned them back on. He swallowed and placed a ham brioche on his plate and dished out a third of the egg casserole. Though the silence continued for a while longer against the background noise of cartoonish cynicism, full of cruelty and stabs of humiliating wit among the rabbits, coyotes, cats, mice, and birds, he finally reached a point of mid-prandial reverie from which he was able to say, "I hear the old man was impotent."

She did not acknowledge the thrust with any sort of parry, as though she knew it was a collapsible stage dagger. She was steady, as she had been at the funeral. He grunted again and shoved the last biscuit into his mouth, wondering where such composure grew, what sustained its roots. Maybe her calmness was due to inadequate nutrition.

While he chewed, she opened the small suitcase she had placed beside her chair. She pulled out a mason jar and a thick folder full of papers. He glanced at these, but quickly looked back at his cartoons as he scooped crème fraiche over his bowl of berries to fill in the corners and complete the meal.

The pale skeleton of her hand pressed down on the folder. "This is a summary of your father's estate." She watched him dip the last half of his biscuit into the sauce remaining in the casserole dish. Then she wrapped her fingers around the mason jar. "And this is your father."

Simeon wiped his mouth with the top of his dirty undershirt and looked closely at the ashes. "Father? There in the jar?" Did she think her words would choke him up, clog his throat like phlegm or rotten fish-pickle? "I will take your word for it."

He poured another cup of coffee just after a coffee commercial came on, and he slurped to dissipate the heat, before testing her. Then he gestured into the air as though he was sweeping his hand before an audience of sapient sameness in the pagan airs of the Areopagus, speaking in the direction of the television instead of Augusta's face, and he made a small speech that he had actually rehearsed in solitude many times, tweaking it along the way. "The long-venerated prompt to contemplative regard for the universe, that great question woven upon the loom of wonder, 'Why is there something rather than nothing?' arrives in our century as a question about why there are realities such as this commercial, rather than nothing. You see, Callimachus the grammarian complained that a big book is a big nuisance, but he never imagined the variety of opprobrial inflictions upon the human mind and soul brought forth through the genre of the *television commercial*. Behold! Two neighbors, a man and a woman, drink coffee of a particularly loathsome sort. To overcome the vileness of their product, the company forced them into a subtle and rather complex relationship orchestrated through eye contact, brief remarks, and smiles. Watch! Obviously, it might appeal to a housewife, for example, wondering if romance has forever eluded her, and seeing here the transient shimmer of possibility. After all, is it not the case that her apartment has a door? Is it not the case that there is a man across the hall? If she were to buy coffee and prepare a cup of the coffee and wait in the hall to be discovered by said man, is there any reason why romance might not erupt? No law of logic would prevent such a thing. No law of nature, nor of the universe in its ethereal elements, would forestall, a priori, the venture of idle lips desiring satisfaction. To the supermarket! Delay not one moment!"

Augusta put down the mason jar and stared at the huge, stubbled face fixed upon the television screen. "Before I left your father's house, I burned down the library."

"One less thing to worry about in settling the estate. Wait! Do you see that?" He reached out and placed his finger on the screen leaving a buttered-biscuit smudge. "That's the new man on the commercial. The first man we have been watching for years is jealous. I feel so badly for him. And there, there! The woman is drinking coffee with another man. Ah!" he covered his face with his hands. He wiped his eyes with his undershirt. "If they don't reunite the first man to the woman quickly, I will never purchase their product again."

Augusta turned off the television and stood up in

front of Simeon's tilt-table. Her hands were folded. Her waif-mop head was tilted to one side.

He placed his plate on his side table and reached for the casserole dish. With the last quarter of a biscuit he sopped up the remaining buttery sauce, leaving naught but orts and scantlings. "What?"

"Your father is dead and you just lie there with your … We have to talk before Gabriella gets here. You can't be naked while I am talking to you. It's ridiculous."

"You can't see anything that is not for public display." This was accurate, because the distribution of his belly provided him modesty since the fat rolls reached down to mid-thigh. He felt secure in the power of portly presence and corporeal magnificence.

Crossing the boundary circumscribed by all worthwhile accounts of human decency she stepped toward him, close to him. He could smell her. The sensation was strange. He reached into his mind for resources to describe her smell in this moment of dread, but he was able to access only the categories of fresh and pure, and then not sweet, and thence not musky, as of the merely pheromonic and sexed, but rather like the bark of cypress, oriental and dark, and he would say the essence of green or of a clean young animal. She placed her hand on his wretched belly but did not look away

104

from his eyes, and he felt a shudder of phallic transformation and submitted to her demand for recognition by saying, "Alas for tongues of fire and the ghosts of books, the flame-licked studded volumes and crops of parchment," as she let her hand slide in the pannus-panicked omphalic direction, and he dropped his hand on hers like the claw in an arcade crane game. He lifted it and felt the lean smallness of the dry hand in the billowed flesh of his own. Here was a threshold as unexpected as it was feared. Who was this woman? The lever of her arm attempted to retract, the only female hand besides his mother's that had ever touched his naked body. "It is time for me to start my work with Jerome the Cuban." As the words left his mouth, he felt the woeful inadequacy of his collection of emergency responses for difficult situations.

Still holding the alien hand, he called out through the open window, his voice pitched to an ox-like bellow reaching past the garden to the beautiful young girls below who were adjusting their chairs and towels and drinks, rubbing oils on their skins, readying themselves for a day under the sun, unpenetrated by thoughts of their own contingency, unshaken by the specter of their own demise, unaware that such smooth curves are so soon destined to succumb to the mysteries of gravity and time. "Jerome! It is long past time that you should be up here and about the work of the day! Jerome!"

"You will need me Simeon." She pulled away her hand and sat down.

Simeon quickly lit a cigarette and surrounded himself with smoke. "For what?" Why were his hands trembling?

"Your brother is not who you think he is."

"That is no surprise. I'm not even sure I'm who I think I am."

"He has become dangerous."

"And I'm not?"

"When was the last time you talked with him?"

He breathed in smoke, and though he had once read that cigarette smoke contains benzene, formaldehyde, acetone, tar, carbon monoxide, and arsenic, he marveled at the way the smoke focused his mind as he thought about Augusta's question and stared at the collection of girls moving about the beach below like Beckett's bees in a hive, a gratuitous mystery about which he too would rapturously say, here is something I can study all my life, and never understand. He knew, of course, that most men unreflectively wanted to penetrate the girls' firm flesh, discharging their interest in a moment, never contemplating why this desire compelled them. What uncurious bores they were. But he was a philosopher, shaped by wonder and speculation. Speculation. Was that not another, perhaps even more invasive, means of penetration? Speculare. The speculum. And he the one spying out. He the menhir of wisdom. Doctor of Philosophical Gynecology.

He felt a piece of egg casserole caught in his stubble and he put it in his mouth. Surely Augusta would soon candidly proclaim that he was disgusting and reconsider her desire to stay.

She continued to stare. Her will to dwell in uncomfortable silence unless she got an answer was Nietzschean.

"I suppose it's been a while." He expelled a gray ghost of smoke with the words while glancing in the mirror. He rather liked the way he looked when he smoked and talked at the same time. The word *cinematic* came into his head.

"Since childhood, right?"

"Never, to tell the truth. Gabriel spent most of his childhood buried in copies of Varney the Vampire. His collection of women's fashion magazines made old dad's malevolent mocking intelligible. Now that he is *Gabriella* not even a god could guess what father's opinion …"

Simeon did not finish the sentence. Augusta's eyes had reddened and moistened at the mention of Gabriella. He suddenly saw that her presence might buffer the toxins from his brother and protect him in a way that was not necessarily physical, but rather in a way related to fortune, like a charm, or a lucky Buddha, or a piece of garlic. Yes, a piece of garlic.

He allowed his eyes to drift toward her forehead, and then to move in a slow descending survey. His gaze was like sap seeping down the side of a fallen tree, until he reached the intersection of her legs, lingered, and then changed the subject. "The chair you are sitting in belonged to my great grandfather. Just in case you want to know, aside from this house itself, that grim little primitive wooden chair is my only remaining artifact from what people refer to as *my family*."

Augusta crossed her legs. The cloth of her pants lay loose about her thin limbs. Dispassion was the mark of professionalism in his chosen art of philosophy. He nonetheless observed, with waxing interest, the pure carnal suggestiveness of the convergence of her extremities, and way she scooted the fundament of her buttocks into the back of the chair in which his own great grandfather had sat while being immortalized in the town's central monument, formed by the gods to stare and condemn the naked, obese, failed descendent that was Simeon. He revered the chair, but had never sat in it because, by the time it was his, he was too big to sit in it. This memory distracted. He returned his gaze to the details of her veined frailty. As he did so, he felt something tip within him, the appeal of weakness perhaps, its smell, or some kind of fear or hope accessible only to the diaphanous soul, quivering and alert. His thoughts drifted upwards, approaching the hovering verities.

Over the walkie-talkie Jerome finally announced, "Agathon, are you coming down or not? I have a box full of tuna hearts I need to salt and pack in jars before they spoil."

Simeon picked up his walkie-talkie. "You are failing me with your solitary selfishness. Fine, then. Cure your tuna hearts in mason jars, Jerome, I am occupied."

"Whelks and cockles of Messene." Jerome was nothing, if not insincere in his marshalling of Simeon's language quirks.

"I have a guest, Jerome."

There was silence.

Knowing that Jerome the Cuban had a speculative mind, Simeon elected to reveal some portion of the truth so that the gardener would not tumble into curiosity and unfounded conjecture. "A friend of my father's." He saw a cringe flash across her face. "A woman, Jerome. So wash your feet and cleanse your foul gullet."

After a brief pause Jerome said, "You are a goat full of lard." Disingenuous servant, mocking his master.

Jerome turned off his walkie-talkie. When Simeon heard the click of rebuke, he turned his eyes back toward Augusta's breasts. They were small, but they had the advantage of being in the room with him. They evoked the ripe loveliness of apples, or better, that of arbutus-berries.

He noticed that she noticed the *Tractatus*. "You would like him. He was inclined toward mortification and the elimination of all human excess and redundancy."

The lack of framing flesh made her eyes look big as they fixed on the photo of LW and then turned to Simeon's great naked belly. Her eyes were calm and still, two balloons in the hand of a child on a windless day.

Simeon licked his large lips. His physical mass should have brought him unusual power. But any hint of power degenerated into the sensation of being stared at like a circus anomaly, wide as a windmill. He chose the way of peace. "Your cooking surprises me."

The slight protrusion of her eyeballs from the lack of peri-optic fat might be enough to account for her look of apparent revulsion. Perhaps she did not hate him for living as an enormous sack of greasy stasis and producing only thought. She might be merely disgusted, without hating. He did not mind disgust. She might not even be disgusted. Maybe she was merely fascinated, like the children who used to stare at him and ask their mortified mothers, *Why is that man so fat?* She might have an inward desire reminiscent of the days when bulk indicated nobility, nobility that was inherently attractive, not least because it indicated the promise of inheritance. He suddenly thought that someone should write a book called *The Phenomenology of Lust*. Such a book would be tremendously useful for a situation similar to the one he was experiencing. Had such a book already been written? Perhaps later he would ask Jerome to go to the library and investigate the question. If it had not been written, what a grand and worthwhile inquiry it would be.

"My father never ate very much at one sitting."

"No, he never ate much."

"Did you marry him?"

"No." The hiss of her whisper was full of a quiet and firm revulsion. She stood and walked around the room with no apparent purpose, agitated like a chick waddling through brushwood. *Like a chick waddling through brushwood?* he thought, wondering at the ways words can both cover and reveal, a *gloss* on some idea being an explanation, and a *gloss* on some object being a covering, menageries of glosses being *glossaries*, little zoos of verbal creatures dressing up, speech about glossa being *glossolalia*, the speech of tongues, the tonguing of speech.

"So, you burned down old pop's library, did you? Come. Sit back down."

"Dress yourself and I will sit. Gabriella will be here soon and we have everything left to discuss. It will not be pleasant." She glanced around the room at the stacks of newspapers, magazines, junk mail, and folded state maps. Her eyes panned toward the television, and then out the window toward the Garden of Memory where the ancient lion was just disappearing around a twelve-foot high stack of curled plastic pipe bound piece by piece with a hundred used cello strings. "Why do you live in the middle of all this strange mess?"

What rudeness. What poor manners. He quickly reviewed the sentences that led to the shift. Was it Gabriella? Or the idea that she might have married his father? Neither of those seemed to justify ruining a perfectly good exchange. "The oddness, mess, and distraction that appear in the world allow me to discover parts of reality I would never have encountered if I planned out all my works and days."

"Just get dressed."

He calmed his inward soul with his usual mantra, *the world is all that is the case*. What an utterly complete sentence. He felt much better, as though he had said a prayer. "If you bring me my pants I will put them on in deference to the swoon of your feminine sentiments."

"Where are your pants?"

"Bedroom floor."

"Where is your bedroom?"

He pointed and turned his television on again. How had he, Solar Magnus, creator of the order of the Garden of Memory, come to this? How does one devoted to reconditioning the human imagination, so that it once again might receive celestial influences, find himself under a female influence, inglorious in the eyes of mortals, interrupting his gloss on garbage, his riff on riffraff, the *sic et non* he was working out with Jerome the Cuban, his trusty assistant, a man who might soon find himself promoted to scribe, though he was excessively inclined toward melancholy, his soul a veritable hecatomb of octopuses, clammy and full of phlegm? How?

He picked up the triptych brochure from the *Universal Church of Logophilia*. Suddenly he saw clearly that which he had only seen as through a glass darkly. Or in a glass darkly. Or was it "mirror," a looking glass? It didn't matter, though he stored away the idea of a glass of ouzo as a looking glass of sorts, turning the mind inward, and then upward toward the eternal verities, or what have you. In any case, here was the place to house the expansive ambition of the Garden of Memory. Could there be any better outlet for the great inveigling, the modern form of reformation? He needed to speak of this matter with Jerome the Cuban.

A pair of jeans as big as a quilt dropped on his belly, thrown by Augusta. "Get ready for Gabriella's arrival."

He loathed the unnatural binding of his flesh and the girding of his stones. A great harrumph erupted as he struggled to pull the pants over the trunks of his legs. This was the dark noon of the soul. His heart was full of a sloppy salacious slush enwombing the embryo of the great thought he might have birthed that day if he had not been invaded. But her judgment was correct. Pantless, he would be more vulnerable to the barbs of his brother's disgust. He was unable to button or zip them, so he accepted unzipped covering as sufficient. He leaned back on his tilt-table and lit another cigarette. "So that's old dad there in the mason jar?"

"Part of him. He asked me to sprinkle other parts

elsewhere. May I have one of your cigarettes?"

He pulled a cigarette from the pack of filterless Lucky Strikes nearest him. She held it between her lips. "I know you don't smoke. The old man would never go for that."

"It's never too late to start." She leaned toward the flame he offered.

"Don't inhale. You'll choke."

She did not cough, and this pleased him immensely and produced curiosity as he poured himself a glass of ouzo, and then lifting the bottle asked, "Two bad habits in one day?"

She shook her head.

"Where did the old man want you to spread his ashes?"

The ash on her cigarette grew and she looked around for a place to flick it. He handed her his ashtray.

"He wanted a pinch of his ashes put in a bird's nest outside his bedroom window."

"Bah!" He yelled like he was breaking a great tree limb with his bare hands. "That doesn't sound like my father." He took a long draw on his Lucky Strike.

"Did he know much about you before he died?"

"Nearly nothing. He would not have been interested."

"Then what do you know about him?"

Fair point.

She took off her shoes. Simeon noticed a couple of hairs on her toes, a detail that he found both appalling and interesting, with an explanation for neither response. He was getting nowhere in unraveling the mystery of who she was. The motive for his interest was curiously opaque even to his own otherwise penetrating mind.

"May I use your bathroom?"

He nodded.

She did not close the door.

He lifted his worn copy of the *Tractatus* and read. "2 What is the case, the facts, is the existence of atomic facts.

"2.01 An atomic fact is a combination of objects (entities, things)."

The gods, or something, caused a sudden convergence.

First his ears distracted him. He heard her urinate. Distraction came not from the pleasant sound, but rather from the thought of the mechanism. He was a virgin. He emerged from a female genital, yes, but he had never again revisited such a site.

"An atomic fact." Anatomic fact.

He listened to the cascade of water from the very place of mystery. The fact of a genital. The meaning of a genital. Love, birth, rape, marriage, whoredom. The auditory experience of the female was disorienting to a man bred on the visual experience of women. Even now, as he gazed upon the bodies of the females down below, he tried to pull together the sense in his mind.

"Simeon, where is the toilet paper?"

"Look behind you on the toilet."

He was instructing her on the location of toilet paper that his own hand had touched. How strange that the sound of urine hitting the water was beautiful. What universal complexities had to coalesce for him to realize that fact. It was musical. A cascade of nature, bestowed to buoy the heart and provoke the exploration of new frontiers in the work of philosophic discovery and contemplation.

Simeon assimilated the sounds of urination, the ocean's waves, the bleats and yawps and shrieks of teen females far below, and farther still the bobbing pearls of tiny shrimping boats that maintained a placid and contrasting calm. His mind drifted to the image of *The Dream of the Fisherman's Wife*, his favorite shunga, a woman enveloped and fondled in the arms of two octopuses, the erotic grasp and suck intensified by the ono-

117

matopoeic thunder-words *zuu sufu sufu chyu chyu chyu tsu zuu fufufuuu* and *hicha hicha gucha gucha, yuchyuu chyu guzu guzu suu suuu*, along with other molluskan examples of cunning lingo.

Questions flooded in waves over Simeon as whole philosophical projects came to mind and life seemed shorter than ever. Merely twenty-four hours before, he was bending his mind around America, soullessness, and the body in general, punctuated by the visual feast of young girls at his feet. Now his ears were as close to the actual thing as ears can be, as any flesh can be. Augusta revealed to him the unclothed auditory world. The knowledge that bodies must somehow mean more than the mere fact of being a temporary coalescence of atoms caused him to ache in new ways. His sinking thoughts moved toward a felt wordlessness, not unlike the means for raising the mind above and beyond itself, a possibility richly explored by Bonaventure, for whom the universe of things was the stairway to ascend into God.

The toilet flushed.

When Augusta returned, she crossed her legs and rested her chin in both hands. Simeon perspired in the growing heat. He stared between her legs, limbs with no redundant tissue, and he thought and he felt and he wondered at what lesson in human vulnerability the gods were planning for him this time.

She sat in silence and stabbed him with her eyes, forcing him to look away from the dread convergence. He suddenly felt lost. He was under attack, playing fat man to Shylock's Jew, inwardly crying, *Hath not a Fat Man eyes? Hath not a Fat Man hands? If you prick us, do we not bleed? If you tickle us, do we not laugh? If you poison us, do we not die?* But outwardly he forged an appearance, cool and calm, serene as a grazing sheep. "So, back to my father. Why did he choose to be cremated?"

"He didn't like the idea of people touching his body without him knowing it."

"He told you that?"

"No one else talked to him. Or listened to him. Not at the end. He had become affected."

"Affected?"

"Not himself," Augusta said. "Possessed."

Simeon sensed an unexpected portal into the metaphysical structure of human and non-human reality, or at least into a curious crevice in the wall of the vague opacity erected by the gods. People who walked by his great house saw the apparent piles of junk through his iron fence, and they wondered at his secrets while they peeked around the edges and gawked through the spaces between mounds of plastic, metal, and rubber. This is why he knew, and knew well, that one can gain surprising insight through the cracks. "Why possessed? Possessed by what?"

"I am 29 years old and without love. I feel like I have wasted my life. I have to move on."

The *non sequitur* startled him.

She stared at the sea. "I need to plan, and I feel safe here."

A tense trace in her voice suddenly worried him. What if he could not extricate himself? "I have to stay here for a while," she said.

The wind was blowing. Outside his window was a flock of seagulls. They hovered in the wind, and when it gusted the flock moved backward just a bit, then forward and down with a dive.

"How did you meet him?" Simeon diverted as well as he could in the moment. Aristotle had already revealed that habits engender action. Thus, never saying no to the wiles of advertisement and the lure of all consumables had conditioned him so that now he was unable to say no to her.

"We'll have time for questions later," she answered.

"Will we?"

"May I have another cigarette?"

He handed her a Lucky Strike. "Are you smoking for my sake, as part of your argument?"

As she sucked in, her cheeks collapsed. She shook her head and puffed.

He sighed with a great heave of the chest, a great flapping and smacking of the lips. "This is my place of discovery. I do my research here." A large burp rose up and he muffled it by keeping his mouth closed. He spoke with phrases rehearsed in solitude. "Conditions in the middle part of a philosopher's life are dangerous and extreme. My thoughts are founded on the basest observations, on waste and refuse. I welcome the appraisal of disgust. It gives me room to work. I am resurrecting the discipline of perpetual return. My home and garden are the incarnation of my mind and will." *Home and Garden*. Why did he have to choose a distracting and benign magazine title while trying to appear dangerous and extreme?

"I can help you. You can make more progress with an assistant." She leaned forward. Her chin rested in one hand, and her fingernails tapped against her sharp cheekbones.

"I already have Jerome." A filibuster might work as well as the more difficult task of clear refusal. "Besides, what I do, my very work, is fundamentally a failure to progress. I ensure for the world that forgetfulness is never confused with resolution. Not many people can understand this. Even fewer can endure it. Least of all those monstrosities whose productive lives emerge in father's wake." His own example was meant to save those who never rest from heavy loads, and who are unacquainted with the sluggish barge of sauntering imagination lusting after happiness unalloyed, wondering which death is easiest, which death best. "Back to my question. How did you and my father meet?"

She stared across his belly. The icons shimmered in sunlight. "He hired me as a psychic."

Simeon rolled his eyes back and reached for a bottle of ouzo. Was she competing with a filibuster of her own?

She stood and leaned across him getting a better look at the icon on the left. "I like this one best. What is her name?"

"Saint Bonaventure." He could physically throw her out if he wanted, but his idea for the book, *The Phenomenology of Lust*, suddenly seemed intuitively important for his overall project, and Augusta was the closest he had ever come to a potential research subject-slash-partner.

"Someone gave him a woman's eyes."

"Do you mean the eyeball, or the eyeball plus the flesh around the eyeball?"

"I mean the eyes. They are like yours, and your brother's."

"I don't believe you."

"It's not something to believe."

"No, I mean the part about my father hiring you as a psychic. Mother used to dig the newspaper out of the garbage after my father went to work just so she could read the horoscope in secret."

"You didn't know him the last decade of his life."

"I didn't know him any decade of his life."

She was leaning over him, too close, sucking energy from some oddly elusive point within his soul, a perturbation he would gladly beat back with his inner staves and knotted straps so that he might regain control of his will. But this seraphic vibration quietly vitiated the legislative output of his active and panicked mind.

"Do you think some people can sense things that others cannot?" she asked.

"Yes," he breathed more than spoke. He then cleared his voice and said, "That is the gift of a great philosopher. The disciplined reception of wonder. We give ourselves over to the unseen, and to the unnoticed aspects of the seen. And so forth. We are quite remarkable."

"I'm serious, Simeon."

"As am I, lady." Confidence began to rally on the distant hilltops of his mind.

"Your father worried that other people sensed something he couldn't sense. He thought his competition might gain an edge on him if he didn't pay attention to this deficit. At first it was nothing more than a passing thought, but it turned into an obsession. Then he met me."

"Ah! Finally! The connection to profit. If you had started with that I might have believed you more quickly. But he wasn't paranoid. Other people's fear gave him a deep pleasure. He craved that pleasure."

"There was more to him. He had a sort of primitive version of a spiritual sense."

"Lust?"

"Close. He certainly wanted to consume and to dominate. But that desire gave him an uncanny insight into his victims. My job was to help him with that."

Exactly as predicted by Hegel's *Phenomenology of Spirit*. "Were you surprised that he wanted to toy with the spiritual through a psychic?"

"I listened and watched at board meetings. I joined him during business deals and social functions."

"You were his temple priestess? Or his temple prostitute perhaps?"

She sat back in the chair and looked down to the floor.

He cleared his throat. "Well, even King David had

his 12-year-old virgin to keep him warm in his old age."

"What if I was his temple prostitute? What would that be to you?"

His imagination immediately filled with the image of a cavern roofed with green boughs, fawn skins hanging on the walls, tambourines and trumpets made of raw ox-hide sounding out alongside the high ting and shatter of flageolet notes, and there in the center of the troubling image his father and Augusta danced naked among scattered trinkets of Dionysian revel, evoking the crave to cave so that even the righteous might gush o're it. "It would be nothing to me. Nothing."

"You don't know anything about sex, do you?"

"It is the lyricism of the masses, if the poets are to be believed. It is nothing to me I tell you."

"That's not true. Your father told me that kindness is your plague and weakness."

"Niceness, maybe. To keep conflict to a minimum so that I have more time to wander the troves of universal memory."

"He said kindness."

"Guilt."

"Kindness."

"Lust."

"No."

"If he said kindness, he meant it as an insult."

"I am staying."

Simeon sat forward on his tilt-table so that his belly rubbed and swayed before her like the hull of a great ship with all the dramatic effect he could muster. His T-shirt did not cover the belly, and thick, black hairs were visible around the callused paleness of the skin making up the navel and surrounding areas. The lines had to be drawn. Now. "No. You may not."

"You are afraid."

"Of what?"

"Of being seduced."

His low grumble was filled with insincere loathing.

"Why would you undertake such a thing with a hunched and bulbous Igor bent over the scraps and leftovers that remain of philosophy?" He pushed his cracked glasses up his nose and wagged his enormous head, a snorting and unpredictable ox.

She put one hand on each of his shoulders. "But what if I wanted you in some way?"

In the wake of her question his great self-righting ship was unfortunately malfunctioning, hull-up, barnacles exposed. He tried to breathe to the side since he had not brushed his teeth. The smells accompanying incarnation had not concerned him for a very long time. "My interests are of the *pragmatico-bacchanalibus* variety. I intend to lie naked, get drunk, and watch young girls on the beach. This is the spring of inspiration for me."

"The house of St. Simone is coming to an end."

"This is a bunch of rot," he grunted and took her hands from his shoulders. "Rot, rot, rot." The house of St. Simeon was indeed coming to an end, but what could he do about it beyond the work of philosophy, incarnating and tending the verities in the Garden of Memory? Why would she even care that no one was left in the family besides a grossly obese virgin philosopher, and a cruel and ravenous transsexed vanquisher in Texan dress? "How did the old man die?"

"I told you. Kidney failure."

"More rot." The phone rang. "I am referring to the manner of his death, the details of his various mortes. Pallor mortis, livor mortis, algor mortis, rigor mortis, decompositio mortis, flammor mortis. These! These are the details I need."

The phone rang and the machine answered it. Once again, he bore the drone of his own recorded voice. Dread clutched at his throat the moment he heard the unhurried force of his brother's low female voice, ruining further an already ruined day. "Pick up the goddamn phone, Simeon. Just pick up the goddamn phone."

In the ensuing silence the machine hung up. Within thirty seconds the phone rang again.

Why this dread?

Augusta's fingers moved, then bent like a rake's prongs and pulled the telephone toward her having just won another chance at victory. Simeon's head hung in weariness.

She waited for the answering machine to come on. The only difference in Gabriel's message was a slight pause between words, like the steps of a man climbing a steep hill. "Pick, up, the, phone."

His dread clutched tighter as he awaited her decision. If she did not answer quickly the machine would cut off his brother again. Who could say what unpredictable shades of misery would fill the heart as they waited for the phone to ring a third time?

She answered. "Gabriella." She said nothing more while she listened. The ghostmask of her face sallowed as a register of whatever nefarious spirit entered through her ear.

In spiritual agony, he placed the fat of his hands over his face, covering the seven holes of his head, darkening and silencing the world as he hurled his will toward the inward places of his mind where he hid the fragments of a prelapsarian remnant, the Theater of Memory that lodged itself deep inside his mind when he first read *L'Idea del Theatro* many years before, an ancient and hidden artifact of universal wisdom that was pressed on by the dissolution of contemporary barbarians until *L'Idea* gave way like an intellectual hernia, extruding into the material world as the Garden of Memory, tended by Jerome the Cuban.

The thought of Jerome comforted Simeon. This fact made Simeon uncomfortable. And yet Jerome alone seemed to understand Simeon's life work. Understand? More than understand. His work clothes were drab, but when he wandered the Garden he often wore a robe of purple, saffron, and green, with tattered hems that created in the sensitive eye the feeling of regal wear.

Simeon sometimes wanted to escape into the Garden below, to descend from his tilt-table and join Jerome in the wooden replica of Camillo's Theater, and to eat grilled fish, which was Jerome's specialty. Jerome had a habit of snapping off a rib from a devoured fish, using it to clean between his yellowed teeth while he hummed a common little Pavan in duple meter. Before he would engage in conversation, he usually had a moment of acid reflux, feigned or not, during which he breathed loudly through his nose, swallowing repeatedly while holding his hand to his thin chest, all of which resulted in the expectoration of a mysterious blob onto the floor of the stage. Simeon would reply in a low, gruff voice, oscillating the jowls and the basket of flesh padding his neck as he shook his head, "You, beard-gathering sir, are disgusting, and you have no manners whatsoever."

Jerome's melancholy gaze would then calm. "Agathon," he would say with no sincerity whatsoever, mocking his employer, "we live in a world that knows nothing of first causes. It has lost the capacity to remember the universe, now that it is dismembered."

Simeon could only grunt approvingly. "But we have the Theater of Memory. We are perfecting and completing the whole with the Garden of Memory."

Jerome would nod, encouraging Simeon to review the well-worn history.

"Though the Theater was once pillaged by Citolini, mocked by Erasmus, and grievously misunderstood by Del Vasto, it was not assailable by mortals. This," Simeon would wave his hand in a grand sweep to indicate the pictures, the drawers of papers, and the gaudy gilded molding around the ceiling with its nicks and imperfections, "this is the skeleton, the very bones of memory, giving form and structure to the mind of humanity. The Theater was not assailable. No, it was taken up as the prophet Elijah was taken up. It was stored in the third heaven. It was preserved among the Ideas until we came along and reestablished it in the world."

He wanted such a speech to pour into living rooms all over the world, counting and countering new varieties of war and pornography, objects available for sale, and everything that felt dissipated and cluttered. Too much clutter. Suffocating. Superfluous. And yet . . . the thousand seeds that die, with only one tree growing, the thousands of sperm that are stranded outside the egg when it shuts down entry, the strange superfluity of Providence—it all gave him hope. The world was lost. Still, Simeon longed to use the theater to recover the divine view of the universe appropriate to humanity.

But the descent into the Garden would have to wait. Simeon was mired in trouble and doom as he waited to hear what Augusta would say to his brother, Gabriella.

She continued in silence as she carried the phone to the window and stood in front of Simeon's tilt-table, staring out with the patient stare of a martyr. Perhaps she was a martyr. Who knew what stories of cruelty Gabriella was crafting for her?

He lifted his *Tractatus* again and opened to the seventh sentence: "7. Whereof one cannot speak, thereof one must be silent." This was no solution for the masses, people who cannot recollect the difference between speaking and silence, whose speaking is chatter and marketing. As the bitter old author of Ecclesiastes said, or should have said, such an effort is a great weariness to the soul, tempting the weak and faint-hearted away from the most important things. Words become slippery. Even what can be said cannot be said. And yet this sentence was the foundational problem of the life of Simeon Saint-Simone, philosopher, for he understood the sentence as no one else understood it. The *whereof* one cannot speak might be passed over in silence when there is nothing of which to speak, or when the reality of the *whereof* is too deep for words, or when humanity has forgotten the language that must be used to speak *thereof*. Which of these three views of the seventh sentence was the truth? Finding the answer was the work of Simeon's life.

He tried to be silent. But the more he tried, the more he felt how little room there was for silence. His inner world was interminable chatter. Even the silence between words anticipated the next word. More to come, as they say.

Ah, but what would LW say? Lean old LW who could not get the logos out of his flesh. Simeon knew—the lingering remainder, dwelling in silence after all that can be said has been said, was the very thing that haunted LW. It pursued him into the quiet of his lonely retreat, into the trenches of war, into the village of imbeciles where he beat hapless students with a stick. Simeon and LW shared this transcendent bond. Yes, yes, good old LW—abstemious, gaunt, hollow-eyed, sitting in his Cambridge rooms nearly empty of books, empty of influence, with a stack of detective magazines in the corner, and music, and young men who . . .

Augusta dropped the phone. In the whoosh of his gasp Simeon's thoughts slipped like silver fish into a dark recess, and the unenchanted outer world coalesced.

She picked up the phone and set it on the table. "He will be here, but later than he thought."

"You didn't say much." He clicked the remote. The Jerry Springer show was on. The topic was *Klanfrontation*.

"He is not happy. You will not want to be alone with him."

Simeon let his head hang forward without turning his eyes from the television. He snorted once more, then surrendered. "You can stay, but only until all this is finished. You're right. I probably shouldn't be alone now— the trauma of father dying and all that."

She slipped the *Tractatus* from his hand and rubbed

134

her fingers over the picture of LW on the cover of the book. "This man." She traced the circumference of his picture as though she could feel some clue there on his sad face. "He looks like someone took this photo just after telling him his father died."

"Karl? No, not old Karl. He's not the reason—or at least his death isn't the reason."

She opened the book and read the first sentence out loud. "*One. The world is everything that is the case.*" Then she flipped to the last sentence. "*Seven. Whereof one cannot speak, thereof one must be silent.*" She closed the book and looked at Simeon. "Seven sentences? What sort of life got him from the first sentence to the last, I wonder?"

"One marked by guilt."

She smelled the book with a deep breath. "He numbers his sentences. Did he believe in God?"

"No. He stopped believing in God. But he continued to believe in confession."

"Maybe that's what he meant by the last sentence." She turned her back to him as she thumbed through the book. "Maybe he knew that some things cannot be confessed."

"He went to school with Hitler as a boy."

"Did they know each other?"

"I doubt it. LW was advanced a grade and Hitler was held back. His family was one of the wealthiest families in Europe. He tended to stammer, so I think Hitler would have despised him. Of course, he despised himself."

"Why seven?"

"It's a venerable number." A commercial came on the television. He picked up his walkie-talkie. "Jerome! Are you there? Jerome! Where are you? Jerome!"

After a few moments, Jerome the Cuban answered. His voice was flat and morose, as though reluctantly reading his line from a script. "Toadying fat-licking dog-flies," he said, with no authenticity of inflection. "I am here, I am here, I am here."

"Tell us about the number seven."

Jerome let out a sigh. Simeon placed the walkie-talkie on his belly and opened another pack of cigarettes while the cigarette he was smoking still hung from his fleshy lips, ashes falling onto his undershirt. Over the walkie-talkie came the sound of rustling papers.

"He is holding down the button so we can hear him. He does this when he is annoyed that I interrupted something. He will sigh a few more times into the walkie-talkie."

Jerome sighed again. Then in the same flat script-reading voice he said, "Here it is. A list. A list of sevens. Isaac Newton identified seven colors of the rainbow—red, orange, yellow, green, blue, indigo, and violet. Seven is the atomic number of nitrogen. The number of palms in an Egyptian Sacred Cubit is seven. Buddha walked seven steps at his birth. The seven deadly sins are likewise seven. Can I go now?"

"That is not even seven examples of seven, Jerome. Devote yourself."

"Son of an eyebrow-raiser!" Jerome shuffled more papers and sighed, as though his life was not blessed by the gods beyond anything resembling what he deserved. "Seven is the sum of any two opposite sides on a standard six-sided die."

"One more, Jerome. Come now."

Jerome was silent for a moment. "Seven is the calling code for Russia."

"That will do."

Jerome gave a final sigh. They heard him turn up his television in the background. He too was watching the Jerry Springer Show.

"It's his favorite." Simeon paused a moment as two young female guests exposed their breasts to the audience and then were rewarded with Jerry Beads thrown to them from the stage. "Why pixelate the boobs?" he asked serenely, waving his fat hand in the air. "They spend a whole hour confessing zoophilia, pedophilia, and incest, or else make fun of dwarves, and then they pixelate boobs and butts. Strange world." He turned full-face toward Augusta, noting the placid lack of shock on her face. "So tell me, were you with the old man at the actual moment of his death?"

"I felt his last breath on my cheek."

"And how did you manage to time that?"

"I thought he was about to say something, to answer a question I once asked him."

"What question?"

She flipped the pages of the *Tractatus*. "Tell me more about this Wittgenstein."

"Well, he's dead. I suppose that is rather important." The plastic covering from the cigarette package dropped to the floor. "Now tell me, what was the question?"

"It was the answer that mattered, not the question. The question was off a Hallmark card. Tell me a story about Wittgenstein."

He stared at the young girls below. Finally, something resolved inside him, at roughly the intestinal level. "When LW was ill, toward the end of his life, he visited a friend in New York. His friend's wife bought a new coat, and she modeled it for the reclining, sick Wittgenstein. 'What do you think?' she asked. He looked at it for a moment. Then he reached over to grab scissors, and he cut off three buttons. 'There,' he said. 'Now it is perfect.' Later she reported that in fact she did like it better minus the buttons."

Augusta nodded.

"So, the question?"

She handed the book back to him. "I asked him whether anyone had ever loved him. Like I said, Hallmark. But he didn't speak to me for a week."

"My father angry over a question about love?"

"He wasn't angry. He just stopped saying anything."

"Bitter?"

She shook her head. "As he moved closer to death he started saying, 'There is something I must remember.'"

"And did he remember it?"

"He said it again and again. 'There is something I must remember.'"

"His last breath was a biblical vapor, the last whoosh evacuating a hollow man."

"There is more to it than you know."

"I just sing my little songs of irony." On Jerry's show Ku Klux Klan members and an angry Jewish man yelled at each other while the safe and guarded crowd hurled heckles and boos.

"Your father cut the electrical cords on all the televisions in the house long ago. I didn't mind. I had the library. And I slept on a cot at the foot of his bed."

Simeon glanced at her, but her eyes were fixed on the television. The television audience was shouting *Je-rry! Je-rry!* The Klansmen were enormous. Some had shaved heads, some had long hair and beards. "We're perfectly fine with you living," the leader said. "Just not in the U.S.A." The Jewish man responded, "We will not be moved. I am afraid of no one. Never again, do you hear, never again." He wept with rage as he said *never again.* One of the Klansmen squeaked, "Never again, never again, never again. That's all we ever hear. Can you prove to me that the holocaust ever happened?" The Jewish man jumped across the stage into the middle of the Klansmen and began to punch. The bodyguards pulled everyone apart while Jerry shook his head at the quirks and foibles of the human race.

Augusta said, "He wanted me to keep a candle lit through the night. I had to buy those big church candles. He didn't want to be in darkness, but he didn't want the lights on. Shadows flickered around the room. I listened to the noises."

The Klan became hysterical as the Jewish man struggled against the television bodyguards, trying to cross the stage. "All right. Be back to clean up after this message," Jerry said, as he walked up the aisle and the camera panned the audience.

He controlled the passions of the crowd like a Master of Ceremonies, but he never seemed agitated or disturbed, no matter how violent or sorrowful the participants were. Simeon admired this, and loathed it. When the show returned, the segment called *Jerry's Final Thought* revealed that his own ancestors were Jewish, persecuted by the Nazis. Simeon was filled with awe at the horrific detachment Jerry had achieved. He knew that the ancient origin of this detachment, grown over 2500 years, reaching its most profound form in Jerry Springer, was a single demonic man from Athens: Socrates. Everything was his fault. No one in Athens could have guessed the depths of what Socrates, with his questions, finally wrought in the world. Simeon understood as never before why Socrates' execution was justified. Who else in history brought about horrors of such magnitude as those made possible by the Socratic curse, the gift of irony?

Jerry's *Final Thought* was a potential philosophical genre. When he wrote his treatise, perhaps he would trace a line of human development in the form of a circle connecting four points, combining Camillo's Theater, LW's *Tractatus* solving all philosophical problems, Jerry's *Final Thought,* and his own Garden of Memory. He would pull together the whole in a great intellectual model that left nothing hidden in darkness. He considered how he might draw the idea on a notecard.

Augusta interrupted his meditation. "Your father wanted to be remembered."

Simeon's gaze descended until it rested flatly on her forehead. "You are making this up."

She sat back and positioned her body in a way that

exuded disconcerting confidence. "He also left me his fortune."

A weight shifted somewhere within Simeon's vastness, a weight with a peculiar quality that was lost among the other weights of his soul, as though somewhere deep inside himself, a great balloon that was tethered to his roots suddenly broke free, shifting everything in its way as it rose to the surface. The truth dawned upon him that he was not responsible for his father's monstrous estate. "Everything?"

"Everything that remained is mine. Does that surprise you?"

His heavy jowls fell forward as he bowed his enormous head to conceal a chuckle. "Perhaps there is goodness hidden away inside me yet. Unfortunately, I am ruining it by taking joy in the thought of what my brother will do when he finds out that our dear father left us nothing."

"Gabriella was nearly as wealthy as your father. But I've heard that some of her deals went bad."

"It's not only the money. He will take this as an insult of the highest order. And now there is no chance for vengeance. This is the cruelest thing he could have done to Gabriella. Insult him, then die."

Augusta rubbed her throat and looked around the

room at the books, old newspapers, broken electrical equipment, and empty drawers from card catalogues. "If I can live here, you can have the entire fortune."

"Oh no! No, no, no, no, no. And again, no. I don't want it. I have no time for money. I require just the amount recommended by Aristotle for leisure. My father already guaranteed that when he gave me this house and set up a fund many years ago. Not for love. Just to keep me from returning to his grand mausoleum. But the end was the same. I have a modest, philosophical leisure." He adjusted the angle of his tilt-table and picked up his Wittgenstein, ignoring the drone of the television in the background. "Gabriella will be here soon in his fancy airplane. I will be unhappy in his presence. Distracted. I must prepare."

Augusta stared at the icons, ignoring the occasional furtive glance from Simeon. "May I use your car?"

"Certainly not."

"I need to buy food for the funeral dinner." She stiffened. "After the dinner, I will be free to become what I was meant to be. And I will leave you alone."

"And what are you meant to be?"

"Where are your keys?"

"Tell me what you are supposed to become, and you can use my truck."

She rolled her eyes and then locked his gaze. "Maybe a saint."

He pointed to the hook by the door, then picked up his book and resumed the appearance of reading.

The keys jingled. The front door opened and closed. When he heard no more sounds behind him he turned his head. Yes, she was gone.

He closed his eyes to relish the brief return of peace before he asked Jerome to make him a little snack.

"Coming up," Jerry said, "live confessions. This week: *Honey, I'm a prostitute.*"

4. *Der Gedanke ist der sinnvolle Satz.*

Did it matter if Simeon thought about his morning with Augusta in the quiet of the minutes after her departure? What of it? Did it matter if he wondered at the choices the love-lorn lass would make at the grocery store amongst the raisins, fennel, sumac, cumin, capers, and marjoram? The warmth of the ocean breeze lulled him into a closing of the eyes, just for a moment.

When he awoke, he felt a sudden sense of panic and disorientation. First, he looked down to the girls on the beach, and then he gauged the time that had passed based upon the place of the sun in the sky. He looked around and saw that Augusta was still gone. In a moment of devastating insight into his own vulnerability he picked up his walkie-talkie and called to Jerome the Cuban, "Jerome! Jerome! Jerome! Come up here, thrice-called. She is gone for a time and we have work to do. My temples are badly shaken by ouzo saturated with the star-shaped pericarp of *Illicium verum*, and I feel like I am carrying three heads and about to have thoughts that will not bode well."

There was no answer.

"The portals of my ears are open wide, Jerome."

When Jerome still did not answer, he took his clean pad of paper on which he was to write his treatise, and he scribbled *GARBAGE* and placed a colon ":" and then he circled the word. He scratched out the word. Then he ripped off the first sheet because the start of things, at least, should be perfect. On the new sheet, he wrote *GARBAGE and the FALL:* and stopped. He gnawed on his pen and lit a cigarette. "Jerome! Jerome!" he called again. "Come here, come now, I must have a scribe."

He held the two concepts of *GARBAGE and the FALL* in his mind, feeling the desire for eternity's glint, shining out not from the gold of shook foil but from aluminum foil, foil wrapped around condoms that were premonitions of crusted latex discarded in the dump, the image far from the mysteries of begetting, or the thrill of beauty, the begetting beauty's anagrammic sequence and end—beg, get in, bite at, use—ah, thence from this thought to his newly nimble nubile research program in the Phenomenology of Desire?

"Jerome!"

Eternity gets its muscular hold as the thing that is eternal is lost. Bodies are run through, and they become the agony of imagination.

"Jerome! Emergency!"

And the ones who had run through her body, the

hidden history of sperm dowels running through the body of his Beatrice ... this, this was the eternal loss that throttles. And yet, what besides such agony could yield a treatise worthy of the Doctor of Immortality? What but memory and the anticipation of the others' bodies, the presence of others in the physical or perhaps non-physical space of past desire, ceaseless recourse to friction and slime ushering the imagination further from the primordial grasp of God's grandeur, all of which might be overcome, so to speak, could yield a worthy treatise?

"Jerome! Come quickly! Consecrated crocus morsels, I am suffocating in the cottony web of a lecherous, loathsome, ruffianly hearth goddess!"

The walkie-talkie made a piercing screech. "Can I have a minute so I don't choke on my Rice Crispies? Suck on your wine bottle for a few minutes."

Outraged, Simeon spoke into the walkie-talkie with such vehemence that flecks of spittle flew from his lips and the flabswell of his manifest neckfat swayed. "If you were up here I would lash you with bound and twisted withes from a lusty willow. I've had not a single drinking-horn of wine, and only so much ouzo as to mend the desolation and fiery crackle wrought fraughtly in the shrine of my mind by a grief monger of the sort who delights at the armor-chink of the mighty who would penetrate a pert teen, and who taunted me with the tone of her thighs and the dread hint that she has been accessed more than …"

The back door leading to the Garden of Memory flew open and Jerome the Cuban stood in the doorway, so tall that the top of his head nearly touched the lintel. "Geeze, Agathon, I'm here. What emergency counsel do you need now?"

"Counsel? Counsel? What counsel would you bring when everything we have known in our work—"

"—our wonderful work—" Jerome added, unmoving in the doorway,

"—might be coming under the force of powers beyond our comprehension—fortune, eros, death."

"Abstractions. Don't blubber. You'll be fine. Also, you have a large zit on your forehead, Agathon."

Simeon reached up and felt the pimple on his forehead. Odd, he thought, at his age. "The memory of asses! What mysterious powers are these?"

"I'm pretty sure you should focus right now. It will help. Don't you have a loci or something that grabs you? One of those girls, maybe?"

"A plague of loci upon your advice. All our work is for nought when verities are traded for naughties."

"Naughties? What are you talking about?"

"It is everywhere."

"What's everywhere?"

"The lure of desire, the enticement of female body."

"Nonsense. Want to know why sunrise isn't marvelous to anyone? Because it happens every day. But solar eclipses, now … Those are a source of wonder because they rarely occur. So your theory of everywhereness has to be wrong."

"You are eclipsing the light."

"I am one of the wonderful things."

"The vast court of memory is a large and boundless chamber."

"So you've said a time or two, Agathon."

"Translate it into the magnificent language."

Jerome thought for a moment. "*Penetrale amplum et infinitum.*"

"Ah, the desire for ample and infinite penetration."

"You should have studied more Latin."

"That would have ruined my ability to learn the wordless parts of mind that merely signal with language."

"Psychic penetration?"

"You have been spying, Jerome!"

"Your talk button stuck."

"I fear the valley is about to be flooded with the

dammed-up waters of passion."

"I'd put a finger in the dame, if I were you."

"You are a vulgar—"

"—but learned—"

"—man. I must eat. Prepare for me several TV-dinners, Jerome, and I will put something special in your stocking when Christmas comes. Then come and watch this next episode of *Jerry* with me. It will be instructive and illustrative."

Jerome sighed and did as he was asked, quickly preparing two microwavable TV-dinners, a loaf of white bread to sop up all the liquid from the Salisbury steak mixed with the red, congealed substance of the cherry cobbler, and a tub of butter-substitute, revealing the reality of being *almost like butter*, as opposed to being *like butter* or *almost butter*, the combination, *almost like*, moving the range of entities that populate the category *food* past any horizon ever imagined in the history of humanity. Then Jerome sat in the wooden chair while Simeon lay on his tilt-table, eating, waiting for the action to begin on television, thinking about the complexity of hidden and involuntary processes such as digestion and the degradation of garbage at the bottom of the dump.

He was too distracted for philosophy with Jerome. But he could endure observing humanity's capacity for pain and betrayal when Jerome was nearby. Jerome gave him a sense of security that emboldened him to open his eyes to the most frightening of American realities. People who had had affairs were confessing to their spouses on national television. *Thou shalt not commit adultery.*

Such an ancient law, one that God was apparently quite interested in. Adultery in the movies was certainly common, and occasionally chilling. But this was actual pain being displayed and witnessed. It was like watching a real suicide.

He watched, chain smoking his way through the third pack of cigarettes. Somewhere in his body he felt the sudden decentering of the spouses, the confusion, as though one of the heavy, hot stage lights had fallen on their heads. Did they know beforehand that this was the reason they were invited to the show? Two betrayals at once. The affair, and the confession in front of the voyeuristic eyes of America, the eyes of Simeon Saint-Simone. Why do Americans watch? This is the philosopher's question in the age of garbage. Jerry knew what Cicero had known about being memorable. Cicero said that one must employ places that are well-lighted, clearly set out in order, at moderate intervals apart, with images that are active, sharply defined, unusual, and that have the power of speedily encountering and penetrating the mind—as the image of ram's testicles are to the idea of lawsuit, so is the image of a bicycling dwarf to the idea of foiled desire.

He felt a vague anxiety grow in the sticky atmosphere of sexual possession and suspicion. There was some philosophically interesting horror pushing through the spawn, just out of his grasp. If only he could focus. All ages knew what the ripped body looked like, the body so mangled that it died numb. But the means for the sanctioned observation of spiritual torments were new to humanity. It was indeed a great age in which to be a philosopher.

The front door opened and Augusta came in.

Focus, he demanded of himself without turning from the television. He whispered to Jerome, "This is she of whom I spoke."

"She of whom you spoke?"

"Indeed."

She carried bags of groceries to the kitchen, but she did not ask him to help. Then she clicked back down the stairs to the truck for another load. Soon she brought another arm-full of groceries. Clicking of shoes. Rapid steps. The crinkling of paper bags. Back and forth, back and forth. Simeon was sensitive to all these little annoyances because he had lived so long with only his own noises and desires.

"There must be less clicking," Simeon bellowed without looking away from the television. "Jerome and I are trying to focus on the demise of the human spirit!"

She went toward the kitchen. No response to Simeon. No greeting for Jerome. She disappeared behind the door.

The backstage camera showed the round, pale face of the spouse, presumably waiting to find out why he was called here, looking around at the lights and props and so forth stored in the waiting area, the last happy moment of his life.

They cut to a commercial.

"Perfectly orchestrated horror!" Simeon looked into the mirror on the wall where the image of his twin stared back at his imagination. When the ninety seconds of commercials ended, the spouse was escorted into the room where the secret had already been confessed to the audience, and to America. The spouse would be the very last to know. "For God's sake!" This strained the moral faculty, even for Simeon, who, in his occasional indulgences in which he reviewed the possible ways for humans to torture each other, was conditioned to hold within himself the entirety of human frailty and foible.

Augusta came through the door wiping her hands on a dishcloth. She had taken off her coat and slipped off her shoes. He was again awestruck by how insubstantial her frame was beneath her white silk blouse, accentuating the braless revelation of her breasts—so much smaller than his own—a veritable topos of perky mystery, presumably capable of producing breast milk under the right circumstances, that secret secretion that is food.

Simeon glanced at Jerome. "I am going to faint," he said.

Jerome yawned. "You're a lion cowering before the strength of a fawn."

"Oh the crags and caves and hollows of my soul, how they fill with the sea-waters of passion."

"At least you're already lying down on your tilt-table."

Augusta said, "I'm Augusta."

"So I gathered," Jerome said.

"Do you see what is happening here, Jerome? This makes me want to live. I don't know why. We are watching a tragedy of the sort that once inspired wars and great books. Now it fills up the time between commercials. But I want to live!"

Captions at the bottom of the screen summarized the content of the episode. The climax arrived. The woman made her confession in simple declarative sentences. In the blank horror of the husband's face, Simeon knew that this man did not suspect what he was hearing. "How could this be happening? I should cry for the man, but I cannot."

Augusta said in a matter-of-fact tone, "Then don't watch it."

"How can I understand the death of my culture if I don't engage in it?"

"It's true," Jerome said. "He has to watch. He's a philosopher."

"Why on TV?"

"Because we are televising our own demise. It's a gruesome fact, but philosophy is the most gruesome of disciplines," Simeon said.

"Gruesome," Jerome agreed.

"Jerry faces the chaos of a world that science and logic have abandoned. This poor little struggling working-class white guy—look at him! He is a victim of betrayal and the general trashiness of his pathetic life. The world is incomprehensible for him. He is trapped and menaced and pursued by powers that make no sense to him."

"Trapped. Menaced. Pursued." Jerome shook his head and looked at Augusta. "Agathon is wondering who sang at the little man's nativity. Who sang? Perhaps his mother? Oh for a mother's voice to soothe. To croon, to lull, to wail. Am I right, Agathon?"

Tears came to the rim of Simeon's puffy eyelids. His voice quivered. This was not just because he was drunk.

This was a genuine discovery. Some underlying structure of the world, as made by humanity, and as consuming humanity, was revealing itself.

"I think this is a rerun," Augusta said.

"A rerun?" Simeon whimpered.

Jerome glanced at him, and then looked at the floor to minimize shame. Such emotion was costly to Simeon and not to be wasted on anything but a live event. "She has cruelty about her, Agathon."

Simeon held up the fleshy mitten of his hand as though to say that he was capable of enduring even these trying circumstances. He searched for the anxiety that had concealed itself somewhere inside his body. The feeling seemed to have a particular locus, and yet when he pursued it, the feeling suddenly diffused, retreating into every corner and crevice, escaping his interrogation. It was a contemporary relative of Socrates' daemon that had come to plague him with taunts, but with sort of a French accent.

"A rerun!" he finally said boldly.

Jerome sighed relief.

"Well, so this was perhaps the memory of suffering, history. Does that change anything? Would it be different if, in fact, the entire thing was staged? America thinks it is watching the real thing, live or no. Is that not just as bad as actually watching the real thing? And what makes the soul ugly, vulgar, gluttonous, grandiose, dishonest, cruel, cowardly, and evil? What, Jerome, what shall we do?"

"Beats me."

"Oh the acres of ache and cream-rich deposits unthinkable in the spurting trial of love that is my very heart."

"He's experimenting with desire," Jerome explained, still not directing his gaze toward Augusta.

Simeon topped off his glass of ouzo, taking advantage of the rule that if you top off your drink before it is more than half-finished, the topping-off does not contribute to the overall number of drinks you have had. "Jerome, I failed to mention that Augusta wishes to make me extraordinarily rich by giving me all of father's estate, which he apparently left to her in his will."

"That so?" For the first time he turned in his chair and looked back toward Augusta.

"Augusta was apparently the guardian of clouds, his lonely dreamer."

She said, "You'll understand more when Gabriella arrives."

"Your brother?" Jerome said in his least spirited voice of the day. "Shit. Shrit. And pschiitt."

Simeon held up his hand to calm the already indifferent Cuban at his side. "The Primal Man is flying in today, and we must put on our finest intellectual armor."

"We shall endure."

Augusta said, "Both of you are in danger, and you are distracting each other with your private babble." She walked to Simeon's window and stood with her hands on her hips, her feet apart, back straight.

"She's Vitruvian, Agathon." Jerome grinned as though he had made a little joke.

"But I fear she is right."

"I know Gabriella," Augusta said.

Simeon nodded his head. Suddenly his eyes focused intently past Augusta at the fence around his Garden of Memory. "Oh good God, not now."

"What's the problemo, Agathon?" Jerome asked.

"The Mormons."

"They're back?" Jerome stood and looked out the window. "Our little pair of enthusiasts, all dressed in black and white. They are persistent."

"Augusta," Simeon said, "We will listen to your tale if you will meet the Mormons at the door and tell them to come another day."

She said, "You don't understand. I am afraid."

Jerome and Simeon looked at each other sheepishly.

"Sorry," Simeon said.

"Sorry," Jerome echoed.

She shook her head and walked to the front door. She opened it and yelled to the approaching Mormons, "Not today! We're busy!"

The Mormons smiled and waved. "We'll just come back later."

She slammed the door shut and returned to Simeon and Jerome.

"She's better at that than we are," Jerome said.

"We are pale-faced men, unshod beggars. Except that you are not pale, being Cuban."

Augusta said, "Both of you smell terrible. Especially you, Jerome."

"Jerome is philosophically opposed to bathing."

"Ruins the immune system," Jerome explained.

"But enough of that," Simeon said. "We agreed to hear your tale about father and other things, in preparation for the arrival of Gabriella. Jerome and I are engaged in the science of imaginary solutions."

"'Pataphysics," Jerome clarified.

Augusta glared and then seemed to gather herself inwardly. "He used to pass by our open front door in his limousine. He would stop and roll down his window to frown toward our little house. My mother, Eva Moon,

162

refused to sell her property to him so he built his kingdom around her, blocking sunlight. I was on the porch many times as he seethed from a distance. That is how I first met your father."

"But how did you get to know him?"

"He sometimes got out of the car and asked my mother to read his palm."

"Did she?"

"Yes."

"Interesting, if not quite believable. Unless he was mocking her. Jerome! Why don't we have any artifacts in the garden from the transformative world of palm-reading?"

Jerome's voice expressed the flat agony of one who labors endlessly without receiving due recognition. "Come on, man. We have elephant tusks, gold pitchers, winnowing fans, vials of fenugreek oil, a triclinium, a set of Bacchic wands, and the framed images of satyrs with gilt ivy-spray around the edges. But all I get is complaints."

Augusta's face suddenly hardened as she stared over Simeon's shoulder. "Just forget it. It doesn't matter now."

Had Simeon been a thinner man he might have jumped off the tilt-table when Gabriella's cell phone rang behind him. She answered it with a purring grumble that filled the room. She spoke in Russian with the unmistakable tone of controlled rage that collapsed time and froze Simeon's joints. Her voice was deep, and it rose in steady, disciplined waves from the cave of her mouth and throat, past her perfect teeth, disarming for having in it the history of maleness. Even Jerome, whose face and voice rarely registered the flux of emotion, no matter what the actual content of his utterance, seemed to have lost a bit of color at the abrupt arrival of Gabriella, who had silently opened and closed the front door as Simeon and Jerome softened their conflict by staring out the window at the single cloud hovering above the sea.

When Gabriella put away her cell phone, she walked past the tilt-table and filled the space in front of the window, blocking their view of the sea. Her polygonal physique was almost exactly that of the idealized statue of their great grandfather. The image of her body rose to Simeon's mind against his will whenever he read of Achilles. She said, "Well, brother, you have turned the family house into quite a junk yard."

Simeon looked over to his icons, their peace resolute. But even they could not calm his tensing nerves.

"Piles of junk." Gabriella grinned with teeth so large and even and white against the contrast of her rouge that they looked like plastic teeth from a Halloween costume. "I should have sold this house to someone who would care for it."

Simeon sighed. A rankling in his chest further disturbed the fragile peace. He longed to resist the descent into cowering, but his heart was more craven than the tawny doe, with ominous buzzing in its dark corners, mumbling monosyllables.

Jerome the Faithful, saw the melting of his master's heart. With a dry and colorless drone, he whispered into Simeon's ear to encourage him in battle. "This lady is nothing more than a hunk of uncarved meat. Don't you worry, Agathon." Then Jerome tried think up something encouraging he could say, using Simeon's own stock collection of insults. "Don't take to heart the pompous censures of this yammering, flap-mouthed flax-wench."

Gabriella ignored Jerome, whose whisper was loud enough for everyone in the room to hear. She fixed her eyes on Simeon, waiting for some response, breathing aggressively through her nose. She seemed more than ever like an idling machine. Her only movement was the alternate clenching and relaxing of her jaw muscles, incongruous with the soft shade of eye shadow, the manicured nails, the long eyelashes around the fierce eyes. There was nothing superfluous on Gabriella's body. The boundaries of her body fit her, neither retreating from the world, nor expanding beyond her control. She carried the firmness of her breast implants as instruments of power. Any single feature—her chin, say, or her nose, or her eyebrows—might seem too large, too bold, too much, or even grotesque. But as a whole everything worked together to display power so confident that no verbal overstatements or witty rejoinders dared to show themselves in Simeon's frontal lobes.

"Is there any good reason the Stump is ignoring me?"

Steadied by the presence of Jerome, Simeon lifted his bottle of ouzo, his well of clarity, and he answered, "Yes. There is an excellent reason." He unscrewed the cap and poured the crystal liquid up to the lip of the glass—the taste of a thousand nights, reminding him of the world of thought that was entirely his own, safeguarded by its divine inaccessibility, buried as it was deep in the soil of his brain.

Gabriella looked at him with a laugh, cold and dismissive. "And you know the reason?"

The light of courage began to engulf Simeon's great body along with the warmth of the ouzo now that he had found words.

In a voice that was quieter, more daunting, tinged with disdain, Gabriella said, "I never should have allowed the old man to keep Stump as his legal counsel. He's always hated me. He is the one who is blocking my access to the accounts. Am I right?"

The music to which the young girls pranced about on the ocean's shore below them rose with its familiar lightness, and Simeon felt a divine spark within his mortal body, a boldness of his own. He farted loudly and absorbed his brother's disgust. "I am the logical outcome, the refuse even, of your dominion. Behold your creation." He knew that Gabriella would not yet understand, but Simeon did not care. Recklessness swept over him. "From now on, knock before you enter. This is no longer a family house. It is my house."

"Bravo!" Jerome said without looking up from examining his cuticles.

"You live in a junkyard," Gabriella hissed. She stood like a pillar of Tauromenian marble. The phone in the pocket of her pantsuit bleated again. She turned toward the sea and listened to the caller in silence. Then she interrupted. "We aren't having this conversation again. Go to the edge. The rest is not your concern." She hung up without another word.

"Another small three-thousand-year-old village in the way of your railroad track?" Simeon topped off his glass of ouzo.

"You don't know me, brother."

For the first time she looked down at Augusta who seemed suddenly drained of blood. Simeon filled the vortex of their active silence with a great sigh. The monolith of his brother was energetically unmoving. But this still-life soon dissolved. Augusta sat on the floor beside Jerome with her legs crossed. Simeon lit another cigarette and tried to bury his aching mind in thoughts of the Absolute. His mind would not cooperate, so he blurted out, with a last puff off the cigarette, "The answer to your question is 'No'."

"What question?"

"About his estate—father's." He pointed to the Mason jar. "That's him, there on the table."

Gabriella glanced toward the jar. "So who told the Stump to cut my access to the accounts?" Then Gabriella looked at Augusta whose eyes were closed, one hand on each knee. Gabriella hissed, "No."

Augusta answered, "Yes," without opening her eyes.

Gabriella lifted the jar of ashes to the light. She did not say anything. She just stared at them.

At least Simeon had the full view of his window again. He reached down under his great belly and adjusted his pants to accommodate the swoon of his mid-section. This was his home, his Garden of Memory. The sound of the squealing girls in tiny bikinis deeply comforted him, bouncing as they played volleyball, unmindful of the cumulative agonies of the world, protecting him from the dulling silence of his brother contemplating the wonder of their powerful father contained in a jar made for pickles. Did that thought not give Gabriella some small philosophical pause?

She put down the jar and breathed deeply through her magnificent nose. It was shaped exactly like Simeon's. She hovered at the edge of her obese and unshaven brother who reclined at an angle on his tilt-table, pants unbuttoned, hairy feet exposed, crystal goblet of ouzo half empty. "Simeon, are you ever afraid?" She looked at Simeon with winter-gray in her eyes, devoid of fear or shame. This was a question offered by a deity to a mortal man, as though from a perverse curiosity.

"Never," Simeon answered in his own best god-like grumble. "Never," he said again as he caught the tail-end of an encouraging nod from Jerome. He was fairly certain that when fear was defined in a very exact way, this statement was quite true. Perhaps he had experienced something that might be *mistaken* for honest fear, some sort of degenerate form of the fear humans once felt in a time when they also felt honest joy. Yes, he began each day with a recital of guilt. Yes, this was followed by resolutions of various sorts, unsupported by faith, but shored up by thoughts of cancer, heart disease, and madness. Yes, the resolutions were then quickly defeated by temptation, the devouring of a cigarette, and the compensatory relief of a craving that substituted for joy, and worry that substituted for fear, balancing in the moment the uneasy weight of the thought of an early death. This? Oh yes, this he experienced a hundred times in a day. But fear, properly defined? He grumbled a third time, "Never."

Gabriella walked behind the tilt-table. She leaned forward, and whispered into Simeon's ear so that the breath blew the small hairs growing from the canal, "Neither am I." Her phone rang and she answered in Russian.

Simeon listened to the low hum of her voice as she wound her way through the labyrinth of business that must have been at the start of each journey leading finally to every piece of waste Simeon had collected and arranged in his Garden. She slid from one language to another, orchestrating her vast world, while from the corner of her eye, she assessed the burnt filaments and string balls of his own little world that appeared meandering and undisciplined when viewed without continual reference to the divine order revealed in the Theater of Memory.

Gabriella pocketed her phone.

Simeon blurted, "Do you know why we're here?"

Augusta opened her eyes like the unmoving cat responding to the lumbering trot and catholic sniff of the oblivious dog.

Simeon regarded the perfect calmness of his brother's face. He knew it was the still pose of a lioness crouching forward, watching carefully the gazelle's final moments of life. He continued, "Augusta is planning a funeral dinner tonight."

"Is the little bird eating now, or does she still only cook?"

Simeon lit a cigarette off the one he was smoking. "How do you know about her cooking?"

Gabriella raised her left hand, rotating the unit of her arm mechanically like a lever, stopping abruptly with two fingers raised in the gesture of a priest's authoritative absolution of sin. "She needs something. She knows that I also need something. As for you, I don't know why you're here."

Simeon recollected the gesture from adolescence, where its imitation of ritual authority was even more obscene. It brought a strange feeling to his chest, as though he forgot his own name. "Everyone can use a little closure," he said.

"This self-starved creature on your floor—don't be fooled. She's hungrier than me in some ways. And I am hungrier than you." The left hand returned to her back. "What about you, Jerome? What part do you play in this farce?"

"Don't count on that." Simeon interrupted before Jerome could speak. "My throat and belly invite myth-making."

Jerome wedged in. "Me? I mitigate hullabaloos and ameliorate brouhahas while tracking similitudes and exempla for posterity. As they say."

Gabriella raised her eyebrows as one in the presence of fools. She put one foot on the edge of the tilt-table and leaned in. Her gray snakeskin boot had a gold band around the edge of the sole. "Battle is always accompanied by hunger," she said.

The boots, the pantsuit, and the eye shadow converged on Simeon. He flushed with the feeling he might have if he saw a beautiful woman, and suddenly noticed that she had seven fingers on one hand.

Augusta interrupted, "Don't torment him, Gabriella. It won't help you."

Gabriella fixed on Simeon's eyes buried in fat. "You

must know something about battle, Simeon, from all your reading."

Yes, Simeon did know. He had read Homer, Thucydides, the legends of Arthur, the writings of a few random saints. He knew there is war, and there is peace. First there is one, and then the other. He waited for the words that would come, summoned, to his lips.

"Each soldier is part of something greater than himself," he said at last. "The good soldier presses against a foe who is likewise filled with passion until the moment when the steel blade crashes through the jawbone. Consummate order followed by consummate pain." Homer had become his muse. "Ouzo?"

"You speak like a soldier—"

Simeon was surprised at the compliment.

"—not like a general."

Gabriella was a pillar rising in the middle of a foggy lake, with no hint of how she remained stable against the muddy floor, no hint of what mystery of form or horror wallowed and fed beneath the black waters dressed in the funeral lace of a gray-white fog. She glared, waiting for Simeon's retort.

Simeon repeated the question his brother had asked. "Do I know about battle? I know the abyss, the gray edge, the smoky ridge over which all failed nations, meaning all nations eventually, fall, soldier by soldier, with lessons curiously unwelcome and unlearned. I dwell away from the surface struggle with its illusions of unity—the general's view, as you might say—and find my home rather in the dim light of the particular."

Jerome grunted and nodded genuine approval.

Augusta said, "I will start dinner."

Gabriella said, "I'm only here because the Stump will not return my calls. I need information." Gabriella's phone rang again. Just as she answered the call, Augusta said, "Stay for the funeral dinner or you will never see a penny of your father's estate."

Gabriella raised her hand and locked a look of controlled but vicious rage onto Augusta's pale forehead. Then she began to pace and rapidly whisper directions to a minion in Italian.

Augusta added, "Tonight we talk about the rape."

Gabriella glanced at Augusta with her eyebrows briefly raised, and she grinned a quizzical half-grin. No nod. No pause.

Her mask was an enigma to Simeon, blank of shock, blank of confusion, blank of anger, blank of fear. But her mask was nearly radiant with intensity that felt like a malevolent light.

Augusta went to the kitchen.

Simeon's mind drifted from the quandary of his brother's face to the scorched-earth wasteland that was the terrain of his inner soul after the word *rape* exploded, uncovering a secret dread unidentifiable without a reconstruction rivaling that of Simonides. *The rape?* Whose rape? Rape by whom? Of whom? Weariness descended under the weight of violent words. His tongue was numbed by spirits, erupting between stretches of mind-blank pain, so that he was tipped and sunk in half-sleep, immersed in a cask of wine. *Rape.* He had the speechless mouth of one who knows not the letter Q. Even when he closed his eyes to listen to the tapestry of girl-squeals emanating from below, he felt no relief from the inward scream that was swelling inside him. The only other sound amidst the sear and smelt of phantom flame in his brain was the sound of Augusta clanging dishes, preparing to cook her funeral dinner.

Simeon looked at the doleful eyes of Jerome and said, "How I wish to escape the howling of all that has come upon us, Jerome, this accidental melancholy, sanguine and choleric, imprinted in the dryness of the back part of the brain, this heat of the melancholia fumosa moving the phantasmata, this dry-hot melancholy, this intellectual, inspired melancholy, *inspired*, raped by the gods."

Jerome turned toward the tormented Simeon. "Your brother puts the gal in gall, Agathon."

"I would rather spend my day with fishmongers than be in this position. Oh to have only simple tasks such as peeling the skin of dog-fish, or disemboweling sea-bass."

"You always seem clearer after a little time sitting in the Theater. Want to go? I can get some donuts."

"Not even the seven planets can help with this disturbance, Jerome. I made a mistake pondering my preamble to *The Phenomenology of Desire* just before the invasion of the ravenous. It left me too vulnerable."

"Are you truly beset?"

"I am. And by Gabriel, no less."

"And no more, I'd guess. Unless ... unless there is something else?"

Simeon moaned. "Man's desire."

Jerome picked a coriander seed from between his yellow teeth and offered an anagram to lighten Simeon's mood, while simultaneously affirming his right to grieve: "Mere sad sin."

Despite Jerome's beneficent gesture of solidarity, anagrammic lamentation hovered in Simeon's breast, and he returned with, "Sad men rise."

Jerome absentmindedly shaded his eyes with his

hand and stared toward the sun. "Men ride ass."

Simeon gasped. "That did not help, Jerome! That did not help at all! Go thence to the Theater. I cannot bear another moment of your consolation. Depart."

Jerome bowed his head, chastened, and perhaps slightly annoyed at the dismissal. "I hope this is over soon. We have work to do. Try to not get too befuddled with everything, Agathon." With this he turned and left through the back door, descending to the Garden. As he went through the door he began to whistle *Rose of Sharon*, loudly, without doubt a retaliatory jab at Simeon who was in no state to be reminded of the *Song of Solomon*. Despite such subtle cruelty, Jerome was a gift from Providence, with all the complexities that accompany a present from jealous and irritable gods. Jerome graciously distracted Simeon from the fundamental question of philosophy, the secret question that plagued LW and his brothers: Why not commit suicide?

When Jerome first agreed to be the Chief Assistant Gardener—he had insisted on adding the word "Chief"—Simeon was pleased. He was also relieved when Jerome seemed happy about staying in the replica of the Theater of Memory. The theater was small, which helped the memory artist use the Theater's constructed *ficta loca*, imaginary places pointing toward the higher reality of the spheres of the universe, topped by Paradisus, the home of Beatrice, she who had to die in order for Dante's imagination to reach such heights. The replica of the Theater of Memory was not entirely satisfactory to Simeon. The door was not very thick, and the handle rattled in the hand, slightly loose, made of shoddy materials. The first time he showed it to the newly-arrived Chief Assistant Gardener, he was briefly embarrassed. But Jerome the Cuban, worn thin from homelessness in middle age, wearing a black overcoat despite the heat, stood on the small stage taking in the logic of the whole.

Because Simeon had achieved, through great discipline, the same bulk as Giulio Camillo Delmino, he contorted with any movement to reach toward his cabinet of notecards, or to pick up the blank diary in which, one day, he would write his book. And because of this, Simeon had been wet with perspiration on that day when he first heard Jerome utter what he called *words of prodigal luck*, and he wiped his face with a dainty handkerchief pulled from his pocket and then threw it away in disgust at its abysmal inadequacy. "How I loathe the hot weather." He had sunk into one of the two chairs on the stage, accepting the tenacity of his own sweatiness and discomfort, looking down and to the side, feeling the thick flesh of his neck bunch up between his jaw and collar bone. "Why do you call me Agathon?"

"You don't like it?"

"I suppose I don't mind." Simeon had then raised a finger in the air as his voice rose in a crescendo with a spontaneous tone of encouragement. "Let us, then, consider our work. We must say things about the world."

"Everything has been said."

"Has it?"

"Everything has always been said, from the beginning."

"What a sad thought."

"Not the least bit sad, Agathon, not the least bit." Jerome began to clean mysterious matter from beneath his long and filthy fingernails. "There is plenty of forgetfulness. What can be remembered is complete, but the remembering itself is never finished."

Simeon raised his eyebrows. "How very wise."

"I just told you the solution to the problem of eternity."

"Thanks."

"You're welcome."

"This is no place of ease, Jerome. My neighbors think my Garden is only random wires and pulleys, broken machines, plastic wraps, and department store dummies, with no wisdom."

"It's a wonderful Garden. I'm here to help you." Jerome pulled out a package from inside his coat and opened it. "Look. These are my favorite cream-filled pastries. Do you want one?"

With his mouth full of thick white cream Jerome said, "You are worried that your Garden is too, what? Mundane? Everyday? Garbagey?" He took another huge bite, stuffing the pastry into every corner of his mouth so that his words were barely intelligible, though he was aware of the maturity and compassionate insight in his comments.

"It is not a worry," Simeon answered. "It is the secret. I must discover the internal logic that relegates so much to the garbage dump. I want to put it all into a book, but I will need to draw upon both the portly soul of the Divine Camillo and the ethereal streak of Wittgenstein. It is a task that would make most mortals quake."

Jerome transiently had trouble swallowing as his head swung forward and backward with the arc of a duck lapping water, while his throat made thick cartilaginous sounds.

When he finally got the pastry down, he took the second one from the white paper wrapping and again filled his mouth. "When you are faithful in small things, the great shall follow." He swallowed, and paused for a breath of air. "Great thought makes room for everything. Look at this marvelous Theater."

Jerome was the only person besides Simeon to see it. Simeon looked around the Theater. "Yes, Jerome, yes. The master included breasts, genitals, human oblivion and stupidity, discussions of sleeping arrangements, illness, animals, torment, and even speeches on the invention of the marvelous windmill. We must be prepared to include everything, everything, everything."

Jerome swallowed the last of his pastry. With a bit of white cream on his lip, he turned his head first this way, and then that way, eyeing Simeon, taking stock.

In the ensuing silence both men were aware that

something wonderful had grown on the horizon of their shared lives.

Simeon was warmed in the vicinity of his hippocampus as he recollected his initial encounter with Jerome the Cuban, he who came to a place of walking shoeless beside the ancient lion in the early dawn, moving from morning silence to cicada-like chattering at noonday, lover of verities and grit.

That was then, but this is now, and now his imaginary places included the distinct new possibility that an as-yet unspecified number of men had been upon and within Augusta, releasing the fluid parts of themselves into her. This new consideration was very different from his long philosophical acquaintance with pornographic images in which ridiculous movements and the contortions of faces, wrenched into erotic deformity, preserved the memory images.

He and Jerome had joined forces to explore the depths of the ultimate residuum of reality, *things*, rejoicing in the soothing ambience in which they lived and moved and had their being, an intellectual and imaginative emollient ooze of oil. But Simeon, who wished to avoid no part of *the real*, had to make the sacrifice of exploring images that had devolved into a catenation of rot, fetor, and reek, images that could only be placed in the parts of memory reserved for hell, with sulfur, fire, and pitch.

He tried to resolve the disorder introduced by the involuntary images of Augusta, et al, that were thrust upon him by coaxing his mind toward his memory of the fresco that hung on the walls of the Chapter House of the Dominican convent of Santa Maria Novella in Florence, glorifying the wisdom and virtue of Thomas Aquinas who was seated on a throne much like Simeon's tilt-table, surrounded by flying figures representing the three theological and the four cardinal virtues, with the saints and patriarchs rejoicing to his left and right, and the heretics whom he had crushed with his learning languishing beneath his feet: This, and this alone, was the image that Simeon needed to fix firmly in his mind, perhaps merging the image of the portly Thomas with that of the Divine Camillo, just to achieve the gravitas required to resist the pictorial onslaught of anagrammatical shag-on-slut anglo-tush sultan-hog talon-hugs projected onto the screen of his imagination, transforming inward tranquility into a carnival of writhing clowns and strangers moistly enveloping the lithe and vital Augusta who disappeared into a mound of painted and naked flesh while an elephant from somewhere blew its nasal horn.

Thomas was fortunate to have arrived and exited the world when he did. Simeon had no flying figures representing the virtues. He had only large black flies buzzing around, representing the fierce principles of the free market and advertising, and it was not heretics at his feet, but lovely young women reminding his desire-sick heart that it beats within a dying animal.

Nonetheless the image of Thomas comforted his heart until the jolting moment when his brother ended his phone conversation and turned to Simeon with a look grim and angry. "What part does abomination play in your philosophy, brother?" She nodded toward the kitchen where Augusta hammered against the cutting board with a knife. "How well do you know her?"

Simeon felt a chill settle on his chest. "She makes a wonderful ham brioche."

In another age Gabriella would have been in a position to send Simeon to the dungeon until life seemed worthier of seriousness. She said, "I didn't pay enough attention to the status of the estate in our father's old age. I was occupied. That was a mistake. The old man has now put her in danger, and she has done the same for you."

"I didn't invite her. Actually, I didn't invite you. I didn't invite the jar of ashes either. I was content. Jerome and I are on the brink of a great discovery, a great philosophical uncovering."

Gabriella turned away and looked at the icons. "Your hunger will always lag behind hers. This is calculated, Simeon. It was a funeral dinner that brought us together the last time. She knows that, and she is using it to manipulate you, and to steal from me. From both of us."

Simeon shrugged, and brought to his mind sentence 2: *What is the case (a fact) is the existence of states of affairs*. The existence of affairs—a febrile love-strife toiling with freest *voila*—inevitably becomes a veil of tears, a veil shrouding reality and leaving Simeon lost.

He looked up at Gabriella's eyes. She leaned in close to her brother's face. He could feel the breath from her nose warm his chin, disturbingly. What perfect breath his brother had. No flavoring, no minty cover-ups. And yet it was so clean and warm, an animal's breath. "You have no idea what the nature of her satisfaction is. Simeon, before I leave for my meeting in London I am going to show you why real war is not fit for your so-called philosophy." Her phone rang again and she answered in German as she walked out the back door onto the deck overlooking first the Garden of Memory, and then the beach, and then the vast sea.

The ocean's breeze comforted Simeon even as the

wind carried to his ears his brother's earthy German, one of the languages that Simeon had studied without gaining any fluency. Gabriella's use of languages seemed so effortless. How many languages had she mastered? Did she feel their thick riches? Did she take in their poetry? Or did she shave off her American accent merely to gain leverage with native businesses?

Down on the beach the pretty girls and handsome boys were gathering sticks and placing them in a pile. "Wonderful," he whispered. How he enjoyed watching the young peoples' bonfires. Later, when night arrived and the sun no longer blotted out the stars, under the infinite darkness of the night sky empty except for the flicker of glory granted to the lesser celestial divinities, the oblivious young would continue their life-filled reveling, becoming intoxicated, feasting on roasted meats, perhaps sneaking off for a romp in the sand. He witnessed the preparations as a god well pleased.

He listened to Augusta chopping, mincing, hammering the great knife against the wooden cutting board so close to the long thin fingers. The breakfast she had prepared stoked his curiosity about the approaching funeral dinner, even if the occasion was remembrance of his father.

Augusta. What a congeries of emotion and thought now surrounded that thin little body.

He swallowed the last of his ouzo and allowed his thoughts to change course, like the Greeks in the battle of Salamis.

The whole battalion of thoughts turned back on Simeon Saint-Simone, Ph.D. (almost). Who is this great man? He folded his hands across his magnificent belly and answered his own question: He is the recollection of all of these forms, containing both the male and the female, the aggressor and martyr, watching as all the world embraces something vaguely called democracy. A new thing was needed, a display of consequences, one who conquers the enemy by being conquered. Simeon Saint-Simone, the recollection of all, the consumption of all. He is the Golgotha of this whole, foaming forth to God His own Infinitude. Three cheers for Simeon Saint-Simone. Simeon was momentarily delighted with himself.

Suddenly Gabriella burst in from the deck. She threw her earpiece across the room, grabbed the overnight case she had set down in the middle of the room, and went into the bathroom. A few minutes later she emerged, blustering no less than she had before.

She came to Simeon and bent over him, searching his eyes as though she would gouge them out if she found anything suspicious. Simeon did not move in the presence of this fury, but he was stunned at how prominent her eyelashes were.

"I will kill her." She blinked her long lashes. "If she confesses that you are part of this before she dies, I will kill you too."

Her powerful body rose up like a stallion arching on its back legs, and she turned and slammed open the swinging door leading to the kitchen. As the door swung back and forth, Simeon could see Gabriella and Augusta face off across the cutting table. Augusta held the large cutting knife that was halfway through an onion.

"Everything?" Gabriella yelled. Simeon had never heard her yell.

"I see that you've been on the phone?" Augusta answered.

How could she remain calm while that animal with long eyelashes lashed with such vehement howls?

"You don't even know my goddamn brother."

The swings of the kitchen door grew smaller, and the door came to rest.

Simeon had to strain to hear their voices. And then there was no sound. Either they were whispering or Gabriella had grabbed Augusta's thin neck and was choking her to death. For no particular reason, the thought occurred to him that with a bit of blue mascara Augusta would either look like trailer trash, or like the saints in the paintings at his left hand, or both.

5. Der Satz ist eine Wahrheitsfunktion der Elementarsätze.
(Der Elementarsatz ist eine Wahrheitsfunktion seiner selbst.)

Simeon held the walkie-talkie close to his mouth and spoke in a soft voice. "Jerome, Jerome. I am trapped. Sneak back up. I think they are going to kill each other."

"May guinea worms infest the feet of that horn-strumpet and your buggerlet brother," came the dull response. Was he growing bored with his place in life?

"I am at a loss, Jerome, at a loss. Why am I suddenly so vulnerable, Jerome?"

"You're losing focus because of the invasion." He sounded like a paid counselor. Horrible, horrible.

"We need an entheogen. Something more than ouzo. We need something that delights in order to inspire us."

Jerome redeemed himself slightly. "I'm gonna finish making lanterns for the Garden and then take a nap, Agathon. I suggest you do the same."

"I can't. They will finish their argument soon and I will have to bear their conflict."

"The solution will come to you. Until later, Agathon."

Providence delivered Simeon to America, and there was nothing to be done about this fact. Most of what passed for contemporary philosophy was too thin a gruel to match the deficits of the American soul, but there were dangers in cruising realms of consumption, even though his body and mind were not standard-issue.

Who could understand discoveries from the laboratory of Simeon Saint-Simone? He was so close to understanding how the verb "consume" became the pervasive identity of the human being, the consumer. This horizon of activity was new on the face of the earth. It subordinated everything to the single and unifying goal of consumption—life, death, suffering, the promise of plenty, the capacity for hope. If he pursued his Doctor of Immortality and started his church, this would be the topic his first sermon.

Augusta and Gabriella were quiet. He briefly wondered if he should intervene. Instead he clicked the remote and turned to his favorite television channel, The Marketing Channel, where Providence spoke to him with the greatest regularity. A woman and a man with bodies that looked as hard as a mannequin's discussed the miraculous next offer: a weight loss program with no drugs, no exercises, no restrictions on what may eaten nor on how much, and all for three monthly installments of $39.99. Feel better, sleep better, look better. Is there a special someone you want to impress? During the long summer months, do you avoid pool parties so you don't have to take off your shirt? Call now! Don't wait another minute. Weight loss has never been easier. I lost fifty pounds in four weeks, and I feel great! You owe it to yourself. If you are not fully satisfied in thirty days, return the package for a full refund. Certain restrictions apply.

Fully Satisfied. What could it mean to be fully satisfied? What would have to happen? What would a person do after this occurred?

He needed to write down the number. He found his pen but no paper. Where was his paper?

Gabriella emerged from the kitchen and stood behind him.

Augusta opened the kitchen door and said in a calm but firm voice, "We're not talking about your problem until the funeral dinner." Then she let go, and the swinging door whooshed a couple of times.

Simeon's imagination pictured the last waves of a dying butterfly's wings, and he distracted himself from the image by writing the number for the weight loss program on the back of his hand, pressing the pen tip into the soft flesh, a butter knife in putty.

Gabriella walked to the back door and grabbed the door handle. She looked toward Simeon with a bleached grin before opening the door and going down the steps to the Garden of Memory.

Simeon reached for the phone and quickly called the number on the back of his hand. A very enthusiastic person answered. He told her what he wanted, and he told the stranger his credit card number, which he had memorized. When he hung up the phone he felt the familiar brief emptiness that accompanied him whenever he bought things impulsively, or when he looked at pornography.

And yet, he thought, this might be a new beginning. He might decide to lose weight, to become slimmer and more attractive. To fortify his resolution—a resolution that was already waning in the predictable way—

he considered standing up and doing some deep knee bends, or twists of some sort.

Just then he saw Gabriella walking in the Garden below, looking out over the work of a lifetime, the arrangements formed only of discard and waste. From his high perch, he could see that once Gabriella turned a corner around the stack of back seats from automobiles made in the 1950s, signifying the mysteries of lost virginity, she would see Jerome the Cuban painting designs on paper lanterns. The orange globes were scattered at his feet. Twenty or thirty of them. Jerome had recently strung Christmas lights along the Garden paths. Simeon had no idea what his scribe was doing, but he liked it. He knew that Gabriella would probe the Mind of Jerome for information and ammunition that she might use in the future.

The chopping in the kitchen resumed. He became aware of a profundity wafting into his Socratic nostrils. His mind wandered wordlessly into an apparent nothingness, and the glass bubble of his mind grew until it had the thinness and vastness of the outer atmosphere, tapering unnoticed into the vacuum of space. What remained, fixed by that delicious smell, was Simeon's great body rooted to the earth, responding like a lab dog with reactive salivary glands. He opened his eyes. His prior resolution was entirely lost. If the commercial came on now, he would not buy the weight loss kit. But he never canceled an order, mostly from fatigue and habit.

He watched Gabriella walk toward Jerome, who was sitting on an old stereo cabinet with his eyes fixed on his paper lantern.

Simeon breathed in. What art could Augusta be wielding in the kitchen? He breathed out. She was a 29-year-old female without love. He pondered their solidarity. Love was nowhere on the landscape of his own life. It was not in memory, not in the present, not in what he could see, hope, or possibly fear of his future.

His hunger was growing, though it was not a lack of fullness. But the aromas coming from the kitchen overcame any sense of satiation. All he wanted was more of whatever she was cooking.

He looked again toward Gabriella and Jerome. As they talked, Jerome pointed toward the replica of the Theater of Memory.

Simeon's mind was suddenly weary of its flight in the rarified air of speculation, and he longed to pursue the alchemy of transforming dead objects into a feast, a true philosopher's stone upon which spices are ground, food as the elixir of life, condiments delectable in cruets, snowy-topped barley cakes, breaded cuttle-fish, cooked prawns done brown, true philosophical gustatory work, a poetry spoken with flavors, a prayer of tongues inspired by the mystical animal corpse wrapped in the seasonings that transform death into food—cardamom, ginger, saffron, nutmeg, and rue—spices of the sort that he would have thrown upon a flaming heretic as she screamed if he had lived in the time of the Inquisition, releasing fragrant smoke to the heavens and all through the towns, breathing in a schismatic essence.

Augusta came through the kitchen door and stood beside the tilt table. "Now everything must cook for a while." She held a bowl with salmon slices sloshing, if Simeon's nose was correct, in vodka, capers, and lemons.

"Tell me about your history with Gabriella."

"No. It wouldn't make you happy."

"Would it make me unhappy?"

"You are vulnerable to desire in a way that makes you vulnerable to pain."

"And you aren't?"

The salmon sloshed. She said, "I am."

"Tell me the story."

She sloshed the salmon and stared toward the ocean. Slosh, slosh, slosh, slosh, slosh. She turned her back to him and looked down toward Gabriella and Jerome.

"What are you cooking?"

She started crying.

He had not seen anyone cry in so many years. He had forgotten how he became weepy whenever he saw someone cry. "It smells very fine. I would sing The Song of Salmon if I could."

She wiped her eyes and moved over to the window, staring out toward the sea. "I love to cook."

"I love to eat dead beasts." He was grateful for the change of subject, but was unable to stop the flow of words. "The alchemy that transforms food into all that a body is, and all that it excretes and spurts."

At first, he thought he might be embarrassed by this last sentence. But he was wrong. It made him feel free. Freedom. The missing thing. All of his Garden and life's work remained uninterpreted. Was there anyone who could understand the thousands of quotes he had collected, tracing the ancient quarrel between poetry and philosophy, the two pillars with an ineffable cobweb strung twixt, a web in which the real secret, inaccessible to either one alone, was writhing? Was there a living person who was worthy of bearing witness to his grasp of the edible parts of the society? And who could give a speech about the waste arranged not only to call the mind back to the history of human thought, as with

Camillo's Theater, but also to provide the prophesy of our demise? Could it be, he thought to himself, that even he, Simeon Saint-Simone, philosopher, had missed the deepest meaning of his work until his massive body met its lean contrary in Augusta? He had much to learn. Providence had obviously brought her to his threshold for a purpose. Perhaps he was indeed ready to listen to the gods speak.

He lifted his eyes. "What is your last name?"

"I wish my whole name was just a letter. Maybe the letter C. It would be more perfect."

"I suppose that is one kind of perfection. But local mediocrity has its place in the larger perfection of the macrocosm."

She looked out the window. "Your Cuban is a strange man."

A subtle shift occurred inside Simeon. Because of his vast size he could almost never locate such shifts precisely. But this one was unique. Of course, he immediately recognized it as jealousy, but as quickly as he recognized it, his great mind rejected the conclusion as preposterous. He was like a chess player who has the advantage, but who must take care not to fall into the trap of stalemate as he maneuvers his opponent into checkmate. True, the thought that he might be ready for love had bubbled up into his brain at the start of his day. And yes, it had been a mildly surprising element in his morning's reflection. But it had probably been planted by one of the hovering gods, a way to trick him into being vulnerable even to such a wisp as Augusta.

She asked, "Where did you meet him?"

"Who?" He tried to keep sulkiness out of his voice.

"Your Cuban."

"At a yard sale."

"What made you hire him?"

"I didn't really hire him. He said that we should work together, and I answered him with my best quizzical look, along with a slight hint of mortification. He apparently took it as a yes because he wrote down my license plate number and showed up on my doorstep. He asked if I had tasks that needed to be done. I answered yes, but I said nothing about who should do those tasks and then I closed the door. The next morning I looked out my window and saw him sitting beside the Theater of Memory."

"You might have called the police."

"I did. But by the time they came he had begun arranging some of my stacks into interesting patterns. Then I realized that he might be put to good use. He could drive my truck and lift things. I would be free to concentrate on the quality of what we picked up and the subtlety of the arrangement in the Garden. So I offered him the Theater as a home. He is the Bruno of Cubans. He is older than me, but he is in very fine shape." He thought for a moment and then he said, "Tell me something. Why does my brother bother you, beyond the obvious reasons?"

Augusta sloshed the slices of salmon in the bowl. "Let's wait for dinner."

"Why are you interested in the Cuban?"

"Do you want to taste something unusual?" She went to the kitchen with the bowl of salmon and returned with a whole pickled eel on a cutting board.

So many years of TV dinners had made his tongue stupid, but it had also made it more susceptible to surprises of flavor. He looked at the eel, the king of all viands at the feast. He said, showing off a bit, "Did you know that it is the only fish to which nature has given no scrotum?" He glanced at her. He was aware of his own ignorance regarding the finer points of seduction.

She cut a small piece of the eel and held it up. "Do you want to try it?"

The eel sliver looked like a slug. "Later."

She continued to slice the eel, pushing the inedible parts to the side.

"Why do you suppose my father put his trust in a teenage girl, a psychic?"

"I was not a teenager." She sighed with a thoroughly unmystical heave. "I will tell you something about the end. He asked me to move his bed near the window. He wanted the window open. For weeks he stared without saying a word. His beard grew. He would not bathe. He didn't want to hear the morning news. And he ate only bread and water. One morning, I was lying on a cot at the foot of his bed listening to the wind billow through his window and into the long hall. Suddenly he blurted out, 'God is light.' 'Light?' I asked. 'Light! Not heavy. Not loud. Light!' He said nothing else for two weeks. Then one day he spoke again. 'That bird. What kind of bird is that?' I pulled myself off my cot and leaned across him and looked out his window. I didn't see a bird. He bent forward slightly and sniffed my hair. Then I heard the bird, but still didn't see it. He relaxed into his pillow. That was when he first said that there was something he had to remember."

Simeon listened in silence and refilled his glass with ouzo. He mused over the venerable process of remembering as she dissected the animal in preparation for the dinner of memory. Through the day the shadow of his beard had grown darker. He sprawled on his tilt-table

202

like a great, bristly cactus, tilting in the desert of his own home, listening to impossible tales. "Are you making this up? That sounds nothing like my father."

"Most of it is true."

"What is the motive behind your tale? It is all detail and no story."

She rested her hands on the cutting board and looked at him. "He never touched any of the money he made. It was all electronic. He never managed the details of the businesses he owned. He bought his mansion for its market value, not because he loved it. He did not know his children. He did not trust his wife. If he gave something away it was for tax-purposes. He never touched a sick person. He never spoke to a poor person. He motivated the occupants of his empire with fear. At the end of his life, I think he wanted to be known by someone. Anyone. He couldn't have that. The walls were too thick and old."

"And so, he hired a young psychic to see through them?" Simeon hid his eyes behind his ouzo goblet. The clear liquid turned him into a cyclops.

"I told him that he was in danger of losing his soul. It didn't seem to surprise him. Instead he said that I had finally told him something trustworthy about who he was. He seemed happy."

"That he was headed for perdition?"

"No. He was happy that that perdition is avoidable, even if he wouldn't avoid it. He could revise his destiny. He chose not to, but I learned something from him. I revised my destiny. This," she waved the knife around the room and the house in general, "is part of my destiny. You are part of my fate."

The day had prepared his heart, unexpectedly, to experience a small thrill. Perhaps she would be the listener to whom he might dictate his great ideas. Had she not spent her life with the stars? Could she perhaps help him sort out the hints of the Sephiroth? Had not Camillo himself been charged by Pietro Passi of dabbling in dangerous magic, of devising a key to the theater which was itself a magical secret? If so—and it was so—Augusta might be the very one, the perfect one for the task.

"I should probably tell you something," she said.

"Yes?"

"I turned over the entire fortune to you before coming here. Gabriella is not very happy right now."

Her words slammed into Wernicke's area in his brain. He slowly realized that he was worth however many millions his father had accumulated. His first response was to observe the faint perspiration at the line between her hair and her pale forehead. The moisture was quite beautiful to his eyes. Then he began to breath more loudly. "Why would you do that?"

"Revenge is sometimes costly."

"How quickly can you have the money transferred back to yourself? Or to my brother? I don't care."

"You're not hearing what I am saying. Gabriella's world is not going well. A few of her business ventures did not go the way she wanted."

"I don't care about money, and I won't discuss it further. What would I do with the money? I cannot watch over the hoards, and the fortune will be stolen incrementally. I didn't like the old man, but squandering his entire life work seems unseemly. If it is to be lost, as it will eventually be lost, as all power great and small is eventually lost, it should be through a force more dignified and noble than neglect, don't you think?"

She looked up. "Was that love?"

"No!" He sneezed. "The money was my father's warchest. He was his money. Warriors shouldn't be disgraced by dying of intestinal parasites. They should die with a spear through the heart. Otherwise a ripple of absurdity mars the texture of the universe. My only task is to master the alchemy of memory and imagination. That is where my philosopher's stone is hidden. Money will distract me from my calling."

"I will be here to help you manage it."

"I don't want to manage it. I don't want to manage anything. I am a philosopher. And no, you cannot be here to help me. You cannot stay with me." Why was he saying this so prematurely? He should stop and think about this first.

"Why can't I stay with you?" She carefully disemboweled the eel while he thought about an answer.

Silence stretched out as he seemed to think, when in fact he was merely trying not to close off any avenues he might want to take up later. He recognized doubt, even when it did not yet wear a name. Then he said something that was despicable, but he was coming to the end of his resources for resistance. "You are not family."

He knew that he had made a tactical mistake when she thrust the sword of a pointed question into his belly. "How do you know?"

"What do you mean?" His parry was weak.

"How do you know I'm not family?"

"That is not a question to be asked. You didn't marry my father. I am certain you will not tell me that you secretly married my brother. What is left? My daughter? I've never had sex." He was embarrassed, but the momentum of the argument carried him forward. "What is left?"

"You've never had sex?" she asked.

How he wished Jerome was present to rescue him. "It hasn't been a priority." The lameness of his response horrified him. "I need bemused detachment in order to retain clarity in my investigation of the phenomenology of desire. You've had sex, I take it?"

She held out her hands, one of which held the knife moist with eel blood. "Many times."

"Many times with one man? Or with many men?"

"Why do you want to know?"

He had long been interested in Xochiquetzal, the goddess of sexual power, patroness of prostitutes and artisans involved in the manufacture of luxury items. This latter point had been useful to him as he pondered which deities to summon as guardians of the Garden of Memory and as guides in his garbage-collecting ventures with Jerome.

"I need to understand regarding the ways my imagination will be tormented."

"Why torment?"

"It might be the case that I am developing a small infatuation with you."

"Perhaps."

He lowered his voice in preparation for a small speech. "Because I immediately see the volume of … the volume, of … milk-cakes flying into the gullet, moistening, a mouthful, swallowed tenderly." He was horrified that the only sensuous language that fully saturated his brain for those situations demanding intense emotional expression derived from his Loeb Edition of *Sophists at Dinner*. He tried again. "I see whirling hot slices of meat flowing on the couches, and the conduits full of piquant sauces, the rivers full of porridge, and black broth babbling through the chambers. I see blood puddings and morsels that could slip easily and oilily of their own accord down the throats of the dead, the rills of hot polenta made of lilies and anemones, and the ever-present memory image for lawsuits from the *Ad Herennium*, ram testicles, scattered slime, creams, and the juice of mallows on the perineum. Oh, oh, oh! It is a burden to have my mind."

"What was it your man Wittgenstein said? Maybe

this is one of those things you can't speak about. But I have a question for you, Simeon. Is it better to be alone in memory, or to risk being judged? Do we love or do we choose to be alone?"

He tried to calm down. "What is love?"

"If you fall in love with me, will you forgive me Simeon?"

"You would have to do something to me in order for the idea of forgiveness to be relevant."

"But you just told me that even the suggestion that I have been with men caused you pain."

"I'm better now."

"Would it make a difference if I was your sister?"

"My sister? Why would you even say that? I already have a brother who is my sister, and I don't like them. So why would you say that?" But she was right in a merely logical sense: He did not know that she was not family. Nor did he know for certain that he was family. Indeed, he knew practically nothing at all. He was hopeless. He felt himself without hope. He was thinking in psalmic refrains. He was drunk at long last.

"We'll talk about this later."

He nodded. He needed relief. He needed to drink ouzo, to lie on the tilt-table, watch the young girls and boys stack their bonfire, and think about the reality of sea, sand, breast, drink, and philosophy, to combat the guinea-worm of virginal desire. What was happening to him? The shades who had circled his world for many years were becoming flesh. He said to himself, "That which I feared has come upon me." This of all times was the proper occasion to draw upon venerable words. He picked up his walkie-talkie and said, "Jerome, put up more Christmas lights!" Jerome did not answer.

The Garden was, at one level of apprehension, little more than arrangements of old household appliances, sewer pipes, road signs, broken televisions, old computers, and military equipment. Without an interpretive treatise, it was nothing more. A wanderer might experience transient curiosity that quickly passed into boredom. But with a treatise, everything would be illuminated, transformed, and unified, carrying the mind past the Garden toward the truth.

When Simeon saw his brother walk around the circumference of the Theater of Memory, he could nearly feel her disdain slip up the stairs and seep under the door as she surveyed the Garden without understanding. His heart quivered when Gabriella and Jerome went into the Theater. At first, he thought this was a wretched development. But then he heard the voice of his brother on the walkie-talkie, and he knew that Jerome the Most Excellent Cuban was allowing him to listen in on their conversation.

Jerome began by giving the standard verbal tour of the Theater, testing Gabriella's limited patience. As Simeon listened to Jerome's monologue, he imagined Gabriella sitting on the old car seat that Jerome had put on the stage. Gabriella did not ask any questions nor say a word until Jerome paused in his speech about the whole. Then she asked, "Do I know you?"

"No," Jerome said flatly. "You do not know me."

"You look familiar. What do you do?"

"I work with your brother on this Garden."

"I've heard."

"The professor is quite earnest in his endeavor."

"The professor? What does he do other than collect junk?"

"He professes. He's paring down the vocabulary of the culture. This is the secret of reading the Garden."

"How long have you worked for him?"

"The gray in my beard arose while I worked in the Garden."

"What did you do before my brother hired you?"

"Hobnobbed."

"Who are you? What do you want with Simeon?" Before Jerome could answer, Gabriella whispered, "If you plan to interfere, I don't play that game."

"I help to keep things straight."

"Stay out of the house. Stay out of our affairs."

"But this is my life now. This Theater. This Garden. Your brother."

She opened the door to the Theater and before leaving she looked back into it. "This place makes no sense."

"The aim is not to make sense. The aim is to discover sense."

Simeon could see Gabriella standing in the doorway of the Theater in silence. "Are you sure I don't know you?"

Then Simeon heard her phone ring. She answered, and her attention was drawn into another world. She left Jerome alone on the stage of the Theater. He picked up the walkie-talkie. After a pause, he said, "An old conflict is brewing, Agathon." He paused again. Then he said, "Your Garden of Memory has become the cauldron forged for the resolution of a great injustice."

Simeon sighed. "Put up the Christmas lights, Jerome. I need illumination of a particular sort."

As Simeon looked out on the evening-quiet of the young who had played through the day, oiled beneath the sun and browning their bodies, unmindful of the leathery or melanomic consequences, Simeon was comforted by the simplicity of the mere body, but disturbed by the challenge Augusta brought to the idea that there is any such thing as the mere body. He was also comforted by the much more stable reality of the taste of ouzo. His weight was three times that of the normal person. His intelligence at least equaled, and probably surpassed, his gravitational superiority, enabling him to think clearly through alcohol levels that would cloud the mind of the average man. His long practice perhaps doubled his tolerance of the molecule ethanol, CH_3CH_2OH, first prepared synthetically by Faraday who was one of the most influential scientists in history despite receiving little formal education. Albert Einstein kept a picture of Faraday on his study wall.

He was aware that his mind was generating digressions instead of doing the hard work of calculating the balance of the evening. In the midst of these pragmatic thoughts he looked down and watched Gabriella walk away from the Theater.

Gabriella had no understanding of the inner workings of the Garden, the machinery of his masterwork. Jerome the Cuban's bones and sinews formed the gears and pulleys of the Garden, while Simeon's great brain and his general sensitivity to waves of cultural change and degradation formed the breath and spirit. When Jerome drove him around town on their periodic missions to retrieve the curbside artifacts of American intellection, Simeon sometimes barked orders, and sometimes urged caution.

Jerome was powerful and able to lift nearly anything. But soon after he arrived, Simeon provided a more substantial means of moving piles by purchasing a small forklift. Directing Jerome from the window was exhilarating, as when gods direct human affairs from above. Or try to.

Through the years Simeon's soul remained the same size, but it was padded by more and more body, a body that carried a sort of garlic, onion, yeasty smell with it. He was ready to concede that this state of affairs left him unprepared for personal change, mired in the bulk of his own flesh, hard to move, with something beyond gravity hindering motion, underscoring his great inertia, an internal principle deriving from the unmoved mover. He was a great ship with a tiny propeller, and an even smaller rudder. Hard to go, hard to stop, hard to change directions.

This is what the taste of ouzo brought back to him, the taste of the beginning, and of the middle. Now if he could only see the end. He drank a glass of ouzo, and drank another, and as he poured the third, he felt the twin in his head beckoning to him. The twin who sees heaven. The twin, like Socrates' Daemon, speaking with a voice like a god since the twin must see the forms and the land beyond the gods.

At the moment he resisted the calling of his twin because his mind was tethered to the image of Augusta's white forehead, and to the beads of sweat, and to a hackneyed comparison with a white rose petal at dawn, and to the hovering mental *non sequitur* beside her forehead: the two highest Sephiroth, Kether and Hokmah.

Simeon had recently been given the insight that the two emanations had been saved by Providence for the extension of his own Garden into the supercelestial realm. In that realm was a coldness and darkness appropriate to the heart of machinery, robotics, automation. He lived in a land of chrome plating, plastic, rust, transience. This was his destiny. So he thought, for decades. Now, however, the very essence of his aim, of his fulfillment of history, had appeared incarnate in the lean flesh of Augusta who would provide part of the clarity he needed.

Of course, Gabriella was also an incarnation fulfilling the history he charted. He groaned inwardly at this thought. Was he denied Kether and Hokmah, and given instead Augusta and Gabriella as their shadowy counterparts? "Is this the great joke you are playing on me?" he asked the gods seated behind the oceanic veil of mist. He was beginning to tire of himself and the mythic ruts into which his thoughts seemed doomed to flow.

He closed his eyes and saw his twin standing in the Theater of Memory with his back to Simeon, shuffling through notes on a table. In his robes he looked like a large decorative egg. From the beach rose the music of Eric Clapton playing *Third Degree*, and the image of his twin swayed in rhythm as Clapton wailed, "I just can't stand no more of this third degree."

Soon, his twin placed the stack of notes back into the vaguely imaged drawer, closed it, and turned toward the living brother. His eyes were steady and penetrating even as his airy body waved beneath them, as though they were the firmly nailed stakes from which his body hung and swayed. When Simeon visualized his twin, neither of them spoke with words, which was easy since Simeon's twin was inside his brain. "The Sephiroth assigned to Venus are hypostatized emanations," Twin said over the music. As he spoke, his groomed eyebrows were raised and the tilt of his enormous head was haughty, but Clapton's controlled lead break may have accounted for some of the grimace of satisfaction. "They are where the Infinite meets the finite, and I can understand why you would want to put them in service to the first twitching in your groin, the same twitch that got Socrates rolling on his way toward eternal Beauty."

Twin sat down with the scant elegance accessible to

one of his size descending into an average chair, and as the opening to *Going Away Baby* started up from the kids on the beach, his little foot began to move and the flesh under his chin wagged as he shook his head and felt the blues.

Simeon's own foot started to tap. Twin began swinging his shoulders more widely and his eyes closed.

Simeon said, "I am becoming a man without understanding."

Twin nodded. "What would Clapton do?"

Simeon shrugged. "I don't know."

"I'll bet that Clapton would do anything, if it would get his baby back."

"Maybe." Simeon was beginning to feel mild embarrassment at the flabby motions Twin was making in his chair as he enjoyed the music. He looked absurd.

"No maybe about it baby. He's found what's important in the world."

"But Clapton has an electric guitar and blues to console him. I have the consolation of philosophy. How do I move a heart with that?"

"You're starting to love this girl, are you? So, what's this jealousy I sense on the horizon?"

In the atmosphere of the blues, Simeon felt freer with his confessions. "All I have is philosophy."

"And the gods. And Memory."

Simeon shrugged. "I will be better off settling the matter at hand and forgetting about love just now."

"You're ready for love, brother." Twin was moving so much to the harmonica solo that the chair began to rock a bit.

"I don't know. I don't know." Simeon held his buffalo sized head and wished both that he had drunk less and that he had drunk more. P and not P. The rhythm of the blues. He began to feel a bit confused as he tried to think his way through the maze to a solution.

"Do you feel disgusted? Do you feel so sad, thinking about the good times you could've had?"

He looked up at his ridiculous Twin lodged in the locus of the gaudy little internal duplicate of the Theater of Memory where Simeon privately stored everything from the highest to the lowest so the entire story could be told. "Yes!" Simeon bellowed and began to cry, and he dug his soft fists into his eyes.

Just as the sound of a slamming door broke through the music Twin's chair tipped and the great man fell to the floor. As Simeon felt a firm tap on his shoulder, he held onto his imagination's Theater for a moment more to see whether Twin was hurt. The last thing Simeon saw was Twin face down on the floor of his internal stage, with his left foot undulating, still keeping rhythm with the music.

He opened his eyes. He looked around him. The door to the kitchen was swinging. He wiped the tears from his cheek on his dirty T-shirt and quickly assessed the damage to his dignity, then assessed his assessment as a sign of his cowardice, then plunged into a tertiary assessment of that last assessment, which left him paralyzed until a splinter of Twin's echoing laughter from somewhere inside his left ear burst the illusory walls and he was involuntarily hurled into the air of freedom before dropping back into his world of excess analysis which kept him from true love. But he would remember the feeling and give it another try later on.

Down on the beach the stack of logs was growing higher. A pick-up truck had arrived with a beer keg and a grill on the back. They were going to have a feast, he thought, a revel, complete with fire, roasted meat, and ale. On the roof of the old pick-up was a boom box. He listened as the music drifted up to him, Clapton singing *Someday After a While*. He felt a kind of relief. The tears had bubbled over and taken away just enough pressure to keep him from coming apart entirely. His own bare and hairy foot resumed its tapping to the rhythm of the lonesome train, to the beat of the heavy heart.

Simeon never thought of his house as made up of separate rooms in which some were private and some were public. For him, all were private. He was not comfortable with this new sense that he was in one room, and someone else was in another room, and that the space of the other room was not freely accessible to him. It was intolerable except for the weight of alcohol, which was growing as the day grew old. It was a day in which a great deal of nothing had occurred. And yet everything about his life was different.

A dish fell in the kitchen with a crash.

He looked over to the ashes of his father. They were nothing. It could be a jar of wood ashes for all he knew. For that matter, everything Augusta said could be a lie.

Only his father's lawyer knew all the details, but Simeon had always been afraid of that short, hairy man who looked like a mossy tree stump. Simeon did not know how to him contact anyway.

How much had his father been worth? The point never interested him. If one is incapable of seeing the beauty of a truly philosophical sentence, wealth is irrelevant. LW knew that. Karl Wittgenstein died on January 20, 1913, and the inheritance Wittgenstein received made him one of the wealthiest men in Europe. But when he enrolled in teacher training college as an elementary school teacher, he decided to get rid of his fortune, which he divided among his siblings.

This would be the model for Simeon, the only model that made sense. Better to give away the wealth so that nothing interferes with grasping a genuinely philosophical sentence, a sentence of the sort Wittgenstein wrote: *The world is all that is the case.* Such a sentence teetered on the edge of a deadly completeness, but LW knew the way out of that trap. What person with even the slightest portion of rationality would contest that sentence? What mystic would refuse to enter the conversation at that point? What politician would refuse to grant that the world is all that is the case? What priest would preach anything outside the bounds of this sentence?

Indeed, with the shiver that often accompanied his true leaps of insight, Simeon suddenly realized he could reduce his world to three things forming a living syllogism: 1) the major premise was the first sentence written in the *Tractatus* by Wittgenstein, *The world is all that is the case*; 2) the middle term was the *Garden of Memory*; 3) and the conclusion was the last sentence written in the *Tractatus* by Wittgenstein, *Whereof one cannot speak, thereof must one be silent.* His life was a Renaissance syllogism.

The back door opened and his brother stepped calmly into the room. She pulled their great grandfather's chair close to the tilt-table, and she sat down so that she was sitting lower than Simeon who still reclined. This was disturbing. She looked up with focused eyes, nearly softened with something akin to pity, the look one might see in a father explaining to his son why he must soon whip him, as though father and son moved in response to a common necessity that both would escape if it was possible. She breathed in through her nose, raised her eyebrows, and prepared to make her statement. "May I have a glass of your ouzo?"

Simeon was so stunned that he almost offered his own half empty glass, but he caught his error in time and instead reached for a new glass and filled it.

Gabriella took a reasonably large swallow.

What had possessed her?

"I have learned that you, Simeon, are now worth 796 million dollars." She spoke almost as to an equal. She sipped her ouzo and let the number hover in the air. Her posture, her silence, the great abstract number—it was all preface to a speech. But the silence was interrupted by Gabriella's phone. She seemed annoyed by the intrusion. "What?" she said in answer when she saw the caller's identification. She stood up from her calculated position and began to pace as she listened.

Simeon had to focus. The topic was money. He knew nothing about money, but he had to learn quickly if he was going to have a man-to-man conversation with her. He translated the money into an idea. Money as idea. 7.96×10^8 dollars. 7.96×10^{10} cents.

Though the sky was far from dark, the bonfire below was lit. What fortunate people these youths were, utterly bodies, not plagued with thoughts about death, fortunes, fate.

He had to concentrate. He pulled himself up yet again from the stupor induced by the stress of the day and the metabolism of alcohol.

As Gabriella paced like an animal behind the bars

of a small suburban zoo, Simeon let each step become a nail in his resolve. He would not let the pacing frighten him, nor the angry tone Gabriella had toward some subordinate in his kingdom. He turned his thoughts about money into a language that did the work he needed.

"No, I don't think you understand," Gabriella said in a strained whisper that forced Simeon to eavesdrop. This was as good as television. "*I* got a call from the FBI. *I* was the one who got the goddamned call from the FBI. If I get another call I suggest that you change your name and take up residence in some place where I can't find you."

She clicked off her phone and breathed through her great nose like a cartoon bull.

Listening to Gabriella was like flicking past channels on the TV. While Gabriella stood thinking about whatever mysterious links were forming into a chain to wrap around her wrists and ankles, the philosopher rested upon his tilt-table and watched the young people below. His own vantage point was ageless and full of grace. He could smell the roasting meats from the beach, unsophisticated but profoundly enlivening. This was an activity far below the cerebral and abstract heights of his own existence, but he was becoming a new man, one capable of envying their simple, fleshly joys. Though he had dreaded this day, he was gaining a new insight into the value of the corporeal world, and of the monetary world, the world of compared value. Money, he began to see, involves an art of translation, the mind expanding to grasp the ungraspable, a monetary philology, a number and kind of power so great that it is yet another thing *whereof one cannot speak.* He should make a definitive list of such things, or have Jerome do it. In any case, it involves the growth of imagination. This was how the gods were converted to humanity.

The number 796,000,000 hung before the furrowed brow of the philosopher.

When Gabriella resumed her seated position, it was clear that she could not so easily regain her equanimity. But she continued like a bad actor. "Seven hundred ninety-six million dollars. Now brother, tell me if I am wrong. You have no idea whether the money is in the form of stocks, electrons in a great computer, private deals, power, or golden coins stuffed into a treasure box."

Simeon topped off his glass of ouzo, held the glass to his massive nose, and sniffed.

Gabriella said, "It's nonsense for you to try to measure a sum that you cannot imagine in any real terms. You will not recognize when you have been robbed of half your fortune. I know you want tranquility. I alone can give it to you."

Simeon lifted his glass of ouzo high into the air and offered a toast to his brother, "You cannot have come from the loins of mortals."

Gabriella's shape seemed cartoon-like now in its un-softened square cut as the shadows of creeping evening smoothed the surface of her clothes. She took off her coat and arranged it over the back of the chair. There was precisely enough room for her in the old wooden chair. The seat was shallow enough so that she looked as though she might spring from it at any moment. She reached over and picked up the *Tractatus*. As she slowly leafed through the book, her calm seemed to grow. "It is true that Augusta, that hungriest of girls, can deliver a feast."

Simeon watched his brother's uncomprehending page-flips, and ignored the irrelevant comment about Augusta's cooking. "In this light," Simeon said, "you look exactly like great grandfather on top of his stat-ue. Except for the eye shadow and the breasts." Art, he thought. Three steps removed from the truth. Just like plastic surgery.

Gabriella ran one palm back and forth along the arm

of the chair with a steady, firm pressure. "Grandfather built this chair himself. Did you know that?"

"Of course," Simeon lied. The bottle of ouzo was empty. He reached down to the nearby case and pulled out another. He lifted it toward Gabriella, but she ignored the offer.

"He designed it so that he would never give the impression that he was at rest. There were two other chairs in his office. Both of them were tilted back just slightly. They were more comfortable than this chair, but anyone who sat in those two chairs felt like they were reclining. The chairs were just a bit difficult to rise from. Isn't that remarkable?"

And Simeon agreed. It was remarkable that anyone would consider such a subtle detail of power so deliberately. It was especially impressive to a man like Simeon who did not even calculate enough to protect his naked buttocks from the eyes of his female guest. "Yes," he summarized.

The sounds in the kitchen had resumed. Augusta was pulling down plates and glasses with a sort of pleasant clinking sound.

"This is all he had at the beginning," Gabriella underscored, as though Simeon might be missing her point. "No jet, no high rise, no chauffeur, no office staff, no tailored suits. Just an insight into power."

The fire down on the beach held his gaze, life coalescing around the flame rising and falling. "What do you think of my tilt-table? As long as we are talking about chairs."

Gabriella glared at her brother's belly bulging from beneath the undershirt. "I don't require much sleep. I can run everything from everywhere, and so I am never cornered. I work on a different scale than great-grandfather could have imagined. But the principle is the same. There is never a deal I must have. It is always a choice. And I am willing to sustain great loss before I will alter that position. This is power. But there is something else I want to talk to you about."

"Do I look more powerful now that I have 700 million dollars?"

"There," she answered in a calm voice. "Do you see what I mean? Already you have dropped 96 million dollars from the sum. If 700 million is the same to you as 796 million, then you will soon have a very wealthy accountant."

Before he could stop himself, Simeon said, "Gabriella, be quiet for a moment." He glanced at his brother. Would she punch him? No. But the raised eyebrows were dangerous. He continued quickly. "I am a fat man, anchored to the only place on earth where my flesh has some history. And from this vantage point, I view whole worlds of thought. Whole worlds, Gabriella. You must fly on your jet to see the various portions of your kingdom. But I merely close my eyes and whole worlds become available to me."

"All of which are infinitely small. Nothing more than ideas. You don't know the size of a real world."

"That is the simple-minded association of largeness with greatness, hardly even an interesting etymological conclusion."

"You sit here in your solitude and watch the world on television. You watch my world on television."

"I have 796 million dollars. Are you cowed?"

"I am never cowed by largeness. It is a discipline I learned long ago."

"Except as it affects others."

"And that is one lesson of power."

"Or evil."

"You surprise me Simeon. Truly. You surprise me."

Simeon took a great gulp from his glass. He was always nervous at the edge of victory. But he held himself steady. "Why do you want father's estate? Do you really need more money?"

Gabriella bowed her head for a moment and thought.

She held her glass with both hands. "Simeon, I departed from my principles. My calculations failed because I was lied to. Not that I'm surprised by the lie. I know the power of a lie. But I made an error when I trusted father. I hate his cremated bones floating in the clouds. I have put too much at risk, and I now stand to lose everything." She added, "Unless I have the money. The estate will save me."

Simeon furrowed his brow. "Am I, for the moment, wealthier than you? Can fate have delivered this into my hand while I sit unmoving, thinking about the verities of the universe? Can tides shift so quickly? Hmmm?"

Gabriella gave a surprisingly meek shrug and said as an unadorned fact, "If I do have the money, I will become wealthier than even I once imagined. In time, I can return the money to you with interest. Or if you want something else, anything, I can get it for you."

Was this a trick, this unverifiable confession?

Simeon had to give some answer now, and he felt the words slip over the arch of his tongue with a life of their own: "Would you be willing to submit to a course of rigorous philosophical discipline in order to earn the money?"

Gabriella looked up at him with sudden fury on her face, and Simeon nearly dropped his drink. But his brother did not yell or hit him, though her enormous hands clenched around the glass. She let her hands loosen, put down the glass, and put her coat on again. "What do you care about?" she asked with the cold, familiar harshness in her voice.

"Everything," Simeon said, "and nothing." He grimaced again, certain that this vagary would undo his brother's self-control.

"I will find what you care about, Simeon, and I will take it from under your nose. And then I promise you that I will choose death rather than giving it back to you. Don't mistake my patience for weakness. That would be a serious error on your part." She leaned toward Simeon, so close their noses were almost touching. "Do you believe me?"

After a long pause Simeon answered. "Yes."

Gabriella walked out the door and back down to the Garden of Memory where Jerome the Cuban was meditating in the fading light. Gabriella had won. Again. Hadn't she?

Simeon breathed deeply and noticed that the alcohol was making him feel a bit dizzy. What was his brother doing? He should have given her the money. Was that not the original plan? To divest himself of worry? To rid his house of the invaders? To return as quickly as possible to the bliss of his prior existence? But even as the thought wafted across the surface of his brain, something clenched inside his chest, and he knew that no matter how foolish his resolve was, he would not give the money to Gabriella. He would sooner choose death.

This thought inspired a poorly located nausea.

He closed his weary eyes and let his mind reach out toward the heavens, the only place now where he felt at home.

6. Die allgemeine Form der Wahrheitsfunktion ist: [p, ξ, N(ξ)]. Dies ist die allgemeine Form des Satzes.

"Jerome, you must come up and watch television," Simeon said into the walkie-talkie. "Hesitate not, and comb not your hair. I see what it is that we must do."

It was time for Reality TV, his favorite genre, and one that included a show that was newly interesting to him, *Lives of the Rich and Famous*. Simeon thought about this fact. Unless he had been lied to, he was now richer than many of the people on the show he had watched so many times. What could he make of this?

A decision was rising up inside him. He felt it and he tried carefully not to disturb it, not to scare it off like a bird on the cusp of his soul.

Perhaps this was it. Perhaps he should contact the producer of the show and let the crew come and gaze upon his vastness and film the spectacle of an enormous man with piles of pornography, newspapers, teen magazines, and a yard full of junk, subsisting on processed food and alcohol, who did it all comfortably wrapped in the sticky silken cobweb of his memory system, changing nothing, but rather bewildering America by continuing his same murky life, only now with three quarters of a billion dollars in the bank, while he contemplated justice and watched the developing world starve on television. Surely that would sell. What good he could do. The fullness of time was at hand, and he felt within himself the preverbal consolidation of a plan, grounded on and rising up from the Garden of Memory, finally providing a glimpse of salvation for America.

He liked it. He looked around. His eyes again wandered to the brochure for the Universal Church of Logophilia. He picked it up. *Yes*, he felt with a certain calmness. This was it. This was the organizing principle he had desired for so long. He had an inkling from the moment that he touched the junk mail. Providence stayed his hand from tossing the brochure away, just as the hand of the Angel of the Lord had stayed the hand of Abraham from plunging the knife into the heart of Isaac his son, his only son, whom he loved.

The ideas themselves that would populate the actual growth of the work in the Universal Church of Logophilia depended on the flesh of his brain for sustenance. Without the ideas, the contents of the Garden of Memory were just so much rubbish and could never be translated into the Message. Nor could the ideas, perhaps, be cast fully in the form of a book since America had moved beyond the Age of Books, and now had a much more ethereal and god-like access to reality through the television and the computer. Perhaps, only perhaps, the ideas should be cast in the form of ritual since that could be televised or posted. He would be the chief priest. Reverend St. Simone. Reverend Doctor St. Simone. The Garden would be the central shrine, the place of relics, the destiny for pilgrims. The book he would write would be the scripture. And Gabriella would be Satan, the adversary. This would deepen the story he would tell on *Lives of the Rich and Famous*. Indeed, the television show could become the means of promoting the new faith. But why one show only? Why not have his own show?

With all the money he now had, the possibilities began to fill his imagination. He lifted a pen from his table and rested the open brochure on his belly. On his pad of yellow paper, he began to answer the required questions.

Name: Simeon Saint-Simone

Profession: Philosopher

Desired Package: Ordination, license to preach, certificate of Sainthood, Doctorate of Immortality.

Preferred method of payment: American Express

Statement of belief …

He gnawed on the end of his pen.

The statement of belief for the Doctor of Immortality had to be 5000 words. He began to sift through ideas, trying to construct the skeleton on which he would hang the flesh of language. He imagined himself with his own television show, perhaps modeled on *The Canterbury Tales*, with one adventure to an episode.

He would model his own presence on The Divine Camillo, but he would not call himself The Divine Saint-Simone. Instead he would use something cleaner and more open: The Divine. He and Augusta could write songs together which would be sung to the hungry world for encouragement. The 5000-word treatise would have to show why memory is critical to redeeming civilization, though there would also have to be the horror associated with memory, horror such as the ache of Augusta's own history, and the mess she made of his inner world. But the treatise was finally bringing some focus and making the mess philosophical rather than merely chaotic. Gabriella might be directed by Providence to mock all of Simeon's plans, but Simeon was the one with the money.

The idea was growing rapidly, growing like an idea pre-made and delivered by the gods. He only needed to write the 5000 actual words for the enterprise to become official. But during a lengthy pause he asked himself, was this really the moment to be doing it? All the distraction might diminish the final result. He wanted to write one perfect draft. No revision. The treatise had to appear at the end of his pen with the certainty of the Decalogue, the heft that only true inspiration bequeathed. His mind made a judgment. The moment was now. Distraction or no distraction. He devised a plan.

Day the first: Talk with Jerome. Day the second: Write. Day the third: mail the application. That was to be the schedule, though perhaps he would start the writing on day the first, just to make sure he finished the treatise.

He picked up the walkie-talkie and said, "Anagram, Jerome!"

"Anagram what, Agathon?"

"Canterbury Tales." He listened to Jerome shuffling back and forth in his slippers on the stage of the Theater. He did this when he was thinking.

"Rusty Tabernacle? A Stabler Century? Bare Lusty Trance?"

"Thanks!"

The details planned and set, he turned his attention away from his religious imagination, and toward the sense of smell.

His vision was intermittently double. He closed his eyes, which immediately made the world spin. Augusta pushed through the kitchen door, flustered. It swung with a swooshing breath, exhaling the smells of food into the room. Simeon opened his eyes.

She grabbed the jar of ashes. "Dinner is almost ready."

Simeon strained to sit forward, and he put his hands on his soft knees. "How can I help?"

She returned to the kitchen without answering.

Simeon put out his cigarette and turned his eyes toward the growing shadows and Christmas lights in the Garden, looking for his brother. What was she doing? Trying to find a way to usurp Simeon's new wealth? Intimidating the Stump? Instructing his lawyers to forge a will, and planning Simeon's demise?

Time was running out. Was time running out? He felt time running somewhere. Almost certainly out. Camillo died before writing his great book. This was Simeon's warning. His ambition had grown far beyond the Divine Camillo's. He had the whole world to evangelize. The scriptures remained to be written. The degrees, the licenses, the television … Everything remained to be done.

But he was mortal! Dread crept up into his throat. How could he get it all done? Why had ambition failed to descend upon him sooner?

He needed help. Could that be the reason for Providence's delay?

Only now was money available. Only now would it make sense to pursue the great goal. And only now could he say that he needed help, and have an actual answer for that need.

He needed Jerome the Cuban, to be sure. But he also, irrevocably, undeniably needed Augusta.

This was a new world, and the new world needed a treatise of its own. He and Augusta were fated to be partners, destined from her first encounter with his father, though, as usual, fate was a bit thin on the details of why it had to be this way.

Nonetheless, never had a thought formulated itself so clearly. She was correct. She was supposed to stay here. She had the advantage of having pondered it for a while. Perhaps this is why Simeon was unable to see this at first. But now he had caught up to her. She had pronounced not only her destiny, but his as well.

He would tell her of his change of heart. He might be cautious, he might set terms, he might stumble over his words. But he would try to say how his heart had changed.

He would force his huge body off the tilt-table. He would strain against the inertia imposed by the day's alcohol. He might even shave the stubble that had grown, and perhaps change the undershirt that had become sticky from sloshes and crumbs and sweat, and that probably stunk to others, though he smelled nothing unpleasant.

He would walk a tolerably straight line, trusting that the words he had to say were forming somewhere in his brain, and he would keep one eye closed to prevent discordant visions from making him stumble, revealing the secret of his drunkenness to himself. He would open the kitchen door, one eye still closed, and he would try to smile at Augusta, while focusing most of his initial mental effort on reaching a chair. He must not stumble. He must present himself as both strong and in need, independent but full of desire.

The enormous effort that would have been needed to do all of this became unnecessary when Augusta pushed a cart through the kitchen door and sat down beside Simeon. She silently arranged hearts of palm and the blood-red seeds of a pomegranate onto a salad platter dense with vegetable surprises.

He lit a cigarette and massaged his knees. His belly cascaded from under his T-shirt. The pendulous flesh hung between his thighs. He stared through one eye like a smelly Cyclops, sniffing gourmet delicacies through undulating, bucket-sized nostrils. For a moment he wondered if his appearance would work against his appeal to her imagination as he made his case for becoming a television evangelist in the name of his new religion. But he had no choice. He had to make his move now.

Her silence was disturbing, so he decided to compliment her in his deepest baritone. "Augusta, you make culinary music. You play fortissimo with fire. You relate your dishes by fourths, by fifths, by octaves. You make me feel the festive lips accompanying Labrus festivus, which can change its own sex as needed. You create platters with marvelous smells of the season, the crane-truffle and the puff-ball, marshwort and celery. I wish to hold whole joints with both hands and bite the flesh off the bone. I want to suck in the subtle herbaceous placenta-like mallow. Polenta-like! I meant polenta, not placenta!"

None of this was what he most wanted to say to the silent, slender Augusta draped in delicate cloth, hair pulled back and up, off her soft neck, her hands wet with olive oil, and her scant presence erupting as a new kind of beauty to his eyes, beautiful in her lack of excess, beautiful in the way she clung to the incarnate world with the fragile rope of her body.

The words he needed to say were rising from somewhere slow as bubbles rising up through maple syrup. He could not hear them yet, but with a few more puffs on his cigarette they would be at his lips. Words backed up behind his closed lips as the light gleamed off her white shirt, and the clean silvers and whites of her colors came into focus. The line of her body was like the stroke of an artist's brush across the dull canvass of Simeon's home. He felt the wild tug of love, and unaccustomed to its lure, he thought he might burst if he did not fully declare himself, embarking on a journey into fog, following the voice of eternity.

She turned to him, hands glistening with oil, and she wiped them with a dishtowel. "The dinner is nearly ready. I will bring the food in here."

"I will call Jerome! He can serve so that you can sit and enjoy."

"I am not here to enjoy. But yes, call your Jerome."

She placed the platter of raw vegetables with the flesh-white and blood-red hearts of palm and pomegranate on one table, and pushed the cart back into the kitchen. She brought cold foods, breads, fruits, and sauces. He could smell the hot foods. His mouth moistened. She brought platters of chutney and egg, mushroom, salmon, beef in wine with spice, onion, potato. Thick food welling up, with subtle surprises. All of these she placed on the card table near Simeon's tilt-table. And she arranged folding chairs around the table.

Blessings upon this woman who weighed less than last week's food. He had to have her. He had to mine her magic for his Garden. He had to tell her what he had learned about masks, memory, and the strange verities circling garbage unnoticed. He had to have, for once in his life, the possibility—whether or not it happened did not matter—the possibility of procreation, the giving of life. He wanted to cry out with desire and surprise. His senses flew to the side as she arrived with a platter of lobster tails. He blurted recklessly, "Augusta, I'm fat!"

He gasped at the stupidity of his confession. He wanted to say that he was afraid, that he did not want her to see him anymore, that he wanted to eatandeatandeat, that drinking could not be stopped or the world might miss the benefit of his treatise, that he was afraid of his brother, he was afraid of the ash-forced memory of his father, he was comforted by his inner twin, he was filled with lust for the generic "girl in small tight bikini" who would have made him panic if she ever took off the ounce of clothing and produced what he thought of as "the opportunity." He wanted to tell her his thoughts when he watched the garbage man dumping tons of waste into the great, smelly truck. He wanted to tell her of his new vision, of his plan to buy a television station and to become an evangelist. But it all spouted forth in the ontological summary of his fatness and showed itself for what it was—a collection of bodiless ideas conjured by a man exposed on a cardiology tilt-table.

"I have already seen how you look." She pulled a browned chicken from the cart, homey and homely.

Thank God he hadn't said everything he thought. Only fatness. He looked at the food on the card table. The smell was complex and delicious, though as he took his second look from platter to platter he was blutterbunged by the fleshiness of the offering from things that once had ears, jawbones, guts, and tongues.

She sucked on a finger that had touched a hot pan. How Simeon wanted to suck on that finger. He would sacrifice all solitude to suck on that finger.

"But," she continued, "you were right. I cannot stay here. I have to let go."

"No! You must stay!"

"I will not." She looked down toward the kids lolling about on the beach, drinking beer, pairing off to the sound of the cyclical sea.

Simeon was glad she didn't look at him as his moon-face reddened and his eyes became wet. How suddenly cool she seemed. *She*—so frail looking, so snapable. But he tried not to deceive himself.

What a mound of food she had prepared. What a day's work. All the elements were arranged a like a single multi-part beast, rising up in the middle with a great belly—the display of torn plants and cooked animal pieces, the sow's matrix floating in cumin and vinegar and silphium, wings from the tender tribe of birds roasted. It was a coroner's slab on which lay the mysterious corpse made of dead cells from earthy creatures with histories reaching back to seed and womb. Soon they would dissect the corpse and taste the inner workings with the wisdom of the tongue.

She looked toward the Theater of Memory. "Does he get cold in the winter?"

"Who?" Simeon choked out.

She turned to him and saw the moistness of his eyes. Her face expressed no obvious emotion. If he once doubted the wisdom of love and the proclamation of love, her sudden coolness made him care neither for wisdom, nor for all the reasons that had clamored for his attention when he was devising his plan to regain his house and solitude. Now he cared only for love.

"Does who get cold?" he repeated.

"The Cuban."

"Jerome? Certainly not. He has a great stove in the Theater. And a space heater. As well as a blanket."

"How long has he been here?"

"Years." How could she care about a complete stranger, and yet so blandly dismiss his great moment of courage? Did she not know what this day had cost him?

He thought for a moment. Well, of course she could not know this. It had to be said. Explicitly said. The moment had passed. Perhaps at dinner, or soon after.

He swallowed and looked at the wine bottles open beside the television. She filled a water glass with wine and handed it to him.

Before he could say a word, a loud gunshot thundered up, and then another. Her face flashed fear, like a hostage negotiator on the brink of success who suddenly hears the shot from the guarded shack and immediately becomes aware of the fatal miscalculation.

Augusta looked out his window to see as much as she could.

The lull after the crack of the gunshot allowed him to become again conscious of the dominant feeling, not in his heart but in his guts.

Gabriella walked in, slowly, quietly, like she had an explosive tied to her belly. She ignored Simeon and stopped in front of Augusta, glaring, her hands fixed firmly behind her back.

Simeon picked up his walkie-talkie and said, "Jerome, Jerome, come forth."

Jerome answered with tearful and tremulous voice, "I will not."

"Why not?"

"Gabriella shot our lion!"

Gabriella brought her chiseled face a few inches from Augusta's. "You think I need to be forgiven?" Her voice rumbled with phlegm, and she raised her hand and firmly stroked her right, black eyebrow with the manicured nail of her index finger, as though an uneasy tension threatening her perpetual equilibrium arose in that spot only.

Augusta's face changed like the first crack of the ice beneath the feet on a frozen lake. Like a poison kiss, she hissed words into Gabriella's mouth. "You never asked."

Simeon Saint-Simone's fluid river of joy become sorrow when Augusta's words solidified into a perfect crystalline moment within his mind, transformed as reality turned into memory, dancing a swirl into a statuesque pose. Nothing about his face or slump betrayed his move from sorrow to jealousy. The hiss from her mouth into Gabriella's, and the steam of their secret and history, revealed to him how distant he was from the family. Even his cold, angry, cruel brother seemed to be connected, if only through hatred. Simeon reached over and lifted the jar of ashes from the table. The lid was slightly loose, so he tightened it and held it in his lap.

Gabriella said, "Why talk about forgiveness? What I do I do. I am the same as you are."

Augusta looked at her and seemed to move from the hardness of her ready attack to the disingenuous softness of the conqueror addressing the conquered. "This is the thorn that must be removed, Gabriel. I am tired."

The disheveled Simeon, mired in the thick jelly of his unprepared body, asked, "Gabriel? What are you saying?" And again, "What are you saying?" He wished he was standing so that he was not looking up at them, but to move would betray more concern than he wished to show.

Gabriella spoke in a cool and gravelly voice, and she bore down on Augusta with her eyes. "Augusta, my dear dove, thinks she was raped. Insists on it, the little mutton. All of this is her revenge. But you have miscalculated, my darling whore."

She grew softer yet. "You are destroyed. Gabriel."

Gabriella eyed Augusta like a lawyer whose client switches his plea after the jury has let him off. And then she grinned, her lips thick with lipstick, her eyes dark with evening shadows. "Do you really think you can destroy me?"

"You have destroyed yourself."

"Your body has absorbed the kingdom's filth. Many men craved you. Why would you worry over one more? Besides, it is my father who is tormenting me."

"In some ways. He agreed to this."

Still looking at Augusta, Gabriella said, "Simeon, what has she told you about her relationship with father? Did she tell the story about being a fortune teller, or did she tell you the truth about her whoredom?"

"Your father said I was gift to him. I believe him. I meant to be a gift to him."

The back door opened and Jerome entered, face haggard with more fury than he had energy to endure. "Why did you shoot our lion?"

The balloon of an image rose from somewhere inside Simeon, and the string hanging from it with a hook on the end caught on his buried clavicle, lightening him. In it, he saw himself bagging groceries at the end of the conveyor belt which brought more and more food. And he was a fat, happy, simple man doing a visible and useful task, arranging things in the bag so that soft items were not crushed and cold things did not abut against bags of sliced bread producing condensation.

Once upon a time, when all was right with the world, Simeon might have prepared four TV dinners and a tray of rolls. He might have watched his television shows and made comments to himself about the state of the world and its variability. But all was not well. All was decidedly not well. The balloon carried him past Augusta and Gabriella locked in cocooned loathing. He floated above his tilt-table and leaned back, a puppet finished with his act until the last scene.

He began to think about the strangeness of the everyday, the strange goodness of the mundane. Two questions in the history of philosophy had laid claim to being the most fundamental. One was Leibniz's question, *Why is there something rather than nothing?* The other was Camus' question, *Why not commit suicide?* Each question was the most fundamental, but the worlds in which each was fundamental were drastically different. And so the most fundamental question, going even deeper that either of these two questions—the question upon which all else depends—is, *Which world do we live in?*

The thought of semen from other men being resorbed into the flesh of Augusta made Simeon want either to die or to erupt into full forgiveness for everything that has caused sorrow to anyone in the world, ever. Camillo died between two women. LW had his boys. And yet they were both concerned with *All that is the case*, and each of them wrote complete, world-containing, very short books: *The Idea of the Theater* and *Tractatus Logico-Philosophicus*. The whole world, with its intensive infinity, had to be made to fit inside the *Tractatus* and inside the *Theater*.

But just when all anomalies seemed fully accounted for, something rose up from the inside of the familiar world causing all sense of completeness to evaporate and tempting the mind to relegate such things to the realm of silence ... the sudden onset of love that finds the pursued beloved already crowded by others, the newborn love consumed like cannibal fish swallowing guppies two breaths into life. And yet, if he and Augusta were alone in the room, there would be only the two of them. There would be no one else present. Only memory. Does memory have such power? Is memory a realm in which forgiveness might actually fail to rescue love?

He lifted a bottle of ouzo, and rather than pouring it into a glass, he unscrewed the green cap and drank the bottle empty. He let the jar of his father's ashes slide down his legs to his feet and topple onto the floor. Then the empty bottle of ouzo dropped from his thick fingers. How he wished he could ask the questions to Camillo and LW. If that were possible in some imagined world,

Camillo would listen on the stage of the Theater of Memory, and then grin and smack his lips, and fold his small hands across the noble expanse of his red-robed belly, and cross his dainty feet beneath his massive legs, a veritable and venerable boulder of flesh.

Then would come a voice from one of the aisles, Germanic, a rough voice, as though the speaker were recovering from a bad cold, and he would say, "Have you ever wondered where the light in this theater comes from?" This would be a haggard-looking Wittgenstein reclining in the aisle, a gray scarf around his neck.

Camillo would say, "It emanates from the ideas themselves."

Wittgenstein would adjust his scarf, and then take out a handkerchief and blow his nose. "No, you see the ideas in this light."

Simeon would ask, "Are these the ideas that make philosophy finally succeed?"

Wittgenstein would answer, "Failure is at the heart of philosophy."

"What dear old cynical Ludwig means is that philosophy always fails to get reality completely into the formula, or the book, or the theater. Better that the mystery of the world be left as a question than killed with a theory. But once you know that, you see that we must try anyway." Camillo would hold up a finger in the air for emphasis. "Pursuing the ever-elusive mystery is the most vital thing! It is this that expands the soul, even though we never finally, completely, get it *right*. Philosophy is about love. If I were to write a book these days I would call it *Imagination and the Value of Metaphysical Pretense in a Created Universe*."

Wittgenstein would shrug and look down at his feet with an expression suggesting that he was, yet again, misunderstood.

"Stop that, will you?" Camillo would demand. "You know I'm right. Take the house you designed for your sister."

Wittgenstein would roll his eyes. "The house. You always bring up the house."

"That's why you are here. To be educated. But you must admit the absurdity of all those boxy rooms and cubical shapes. Too many sharp corners. Do you think she really liked it? A woman?"

"I saw the house," Simeon would say, though he had only seen it in a book. "I liked the design of the windows."

Wittgenstein would nod in appreciation.

"No, no, no. The cure would be much easier if you

had read more philosophy. What would I not give for you to have read more Plato?"

Wittgenstein would allow half of his mouth to grin. "Where do you think I got my idea for seven sentences? Read Plato's *Seventh Epistle*. Read sentence 6.54."

"You were searching for a cure. But if you cure this question-asking, if you cure the dissatisfied human of the longing to pursue the unanswerable, what remains? You should have eaten more. Look at you—all skin and bones. That's why you have this cold. Not enough real nutrition. The philosophy you choked on was too thin a gruel to begin with. Spend more time here in the Theater and I will cure you of your cold."

Simeon knew, of course, about the sickness that must be cured, a new and insidious form of *consumption*, a paralyzing though infinite access to all manner of human expression requiring search engines to perceive preferences, engines made to reinforce the preferences by serving up only those sites—those *topoi*—that fit a soul's immediate cravings. The soul is sold things that reinforce preferences, a totalitarianism of freedom consuming Simeon's future congregation of souls while imagination and memory continue to shrink, causing their souls to disappear into a flash of predictable desire.

The question—the little quest—of Simeon's life became clear: such souls needed to be saved.

"It is certainly warm in here," Wittgenstein would observe. "And wherever the light is coming from, it has a pleasant yellowness. But the molding around the ceiling is bit gaudy, don't you think?"

Camillo would grunt. "Gaudiness is exactly what you need."

"Once you get past the slight mustiness of the stored papers and ideas, the smell is quite wonderful."

Simeon would offer, "That's Augusta's funeral dinner."

"Lovely."

Camillo would nod in agreement. "But you, Ludwig, must start with chicken soup. I will get you some in a moment."

The blended voices of Augusta and Gabriella penetrated the swirl of Simeon's mind, mere sounds rather than words.

Simeon would say to Camillo and LW, "I am in love with her."

The two great men would neither smile nor look embarrassed. Instead, they would nod, men who understood in their own ways. Camillo would say, "She reminds me of one of my beloved ladies in Milan. Oh, what wonderful days those were."

"Simeon," Augusta said as she poked her finger into his side.

Eyes still closed, Simeon would resolutely say within himself, "I must discover the truth by living the questions that lie before me. I must now face the death of my father, the presence of love, and a modicum of betrayal. I need something. I don't know what."

"You need to be born again," Wittgenstein would immediately say, and his face would seem especially somber.

"Ah yes, Ludwig," Camillo would say, agreeably. "And what womb do we emerge from? What incubating smallness of world do we break out of? We experience such comfort in there. But we must be born into the larger world and relinquish our comfort. We must emerge into the larger world, or else die in the womb, for we are not creatures meant for such cocooned pandering to the soft cob-webby surrounds that comfort but also constrict, keeping the wings folded, eventually choking out the life."

The two men would nod again toward Simeon as he committed himself to the funeral dinner with a sense of doom and grave anxiety.

7. Wovon man nicht sprechen kann, darüber muss man schweigen.

Jerome had apparently decided to sit on the floor with his arms crossed and sulk, though that word seemed disrespectful to whatever emotion the Cuban was attempting to express. Silent dread, confusion, and rage thickened the air in the room and made it difficult for Simeon to breathe.

The food arranged on the table was mounded up in the middle and tapered at either end so that the whole looked like the coalescing inward parts of a great body minus the integument. On one side of the mound Augusta placed the jar of ashes that had once been his father. On the other side she placed a bouquet of white tulips like the contorted toes of the old. In the middle of the body were brown meats and white meats, each with sauces and toppings born from an imagination fully sympathetic with the meat's own simple untopped harmony. There were arrangements of carrots bundled in strips of leeks along with potatoes variously crisped and baked. Warm wide loaves of bread with the white inner belly cut open were slathered with sweet butter. She had delivered the meal—pickled, pied, freckled, fried—with the efficiency of a chef on the Cooking Channel, offering the world one lush mouthful at a time. The small table was covered, and it was clear that eating would be the point. Eating and drinking. Though Simeon was not in top form due to the excess of stress and alcohol through the day, he was nonetheless moved aesthetically when he saw a large decanter of scotch and three bottles of La Fleur Petrus Pomerol poking up from the variegated arrangement of dead things.

Augusta, her face tuned to sadness, pulled two folding chairs to the table for Gabriella and herself. To Simeon's eyes Gabriella's eyebrows seemed to have grown though the day and the evening. The boldness of her features was even more cartoon-like, but not with the insubstantial cartoon-like presence, presence with no real and permanent results.

Simeon revised his thoughts about Augusta's face. She sat with an expression somewhere between loathing and beatific concern for the feelings of a sensitive God. But she had created the feast. No money that Gabriella might make, and no book or symbol that Simeon might produce, could be eaten. When does one encounter an idea that can be transformed into actual flesh? An edible idea, incarnation on a small but lovely scale.

Thus could much be forgiven Augusta. Indeed, what had first struck him as sickly asthenia now nearly overwhelmed his ouzo- and love-primed mind as an ethereal approach to flesh, that mystery among the saints that balanced the excesses of Camillo's human wisdom. He knew with deep knowledge—knowledge as it comes to great minds, sudden insight, the sorting out of some unifying equation while tying one's shoes—that he was incomplete, and that no amount of expansion would make him whole. Augusta might teach him, and he might teach her. Here, he thought, was the only good argument for Aristophanes' myth at the Drinking Party. Here was recollection of wholeness. He closed his eyes and breathed in deeply as the sights and smells became like living beings emanating from the dead carcass of dinner. But this, Simeon thought, was not the smell of death. This was the smell of an absolute delight.

Simeon found the strength to sit up and position himself at the end of his tilt-table. He did not wait for Gabriella to sit with her cold, distant presence protesting the leverage Simeon held. He reached out, and with his bare hand he pulled off a piece of the beef cooked to a point of such delicacy that only the desire to prolong pleasure would keep him from eating it all with quick and aggressive swoops of the hands. He took one piece. He placed it in his mouth and let the juice flow from between the individual cells of the muscle. He sat holding in his mouth a piece of flesh no different from the flesh of his own large tongue. He felt the secretions his mouth produced. He savored, and then he swallowed, allowing the secrets of digestion and nutrition to begin their mysterious work. Consumption by itself was not enough. Evaluation was required.

Augusta poured each of them a glass of wine. In his reverie Simeon misplaced his resolution and drank the whole glass. But there was no chastisement. After a brief glance of disgust from Gabriella, Augusta moved in, refilled the empty glass, and put the bottle beside his plate, anticipating his wish. He would sing the Song of Solomon if he had time and memory enough. This time he took a more disciplined sip of his wine and said, "Three bowls only do I mix for the temperate—one to health, which they empty first, the second to love and pleasure, the third to sleep. When this is drunk up wise guests go home. The fourth bowl is ours no longer, but belongs to violence, the fifth to uproar, the sixth to drunken revel, the seventh to black eyes. The eighth is the policeman's, the ninth belongs to biliousness, and the tenth to madness and hurling the furniture. So says Eubulus, and I am inclined to agree."

As he took more food, he was aware of being stared at by Gabriella, and looked at by Augusta. His portions were reasonable. But there could be no *a priori* limit on the number of times he would reach toward the table to refill his plate.

His plate was filled. It was heaping. But this was his house and he had the hunger not merely of a fat man, and not merely of a man who has had too much to drink, but the hunger of one who is reacquainting himself with glory, recovering from an acquired tolerance of processed and potted food products.

In the still air around Augusta and Gabriella he reached for yet another piece of the beef, and instead he found himself grabbing a chocolate, with a glance of genuine inquiry toward Augusta.

Augusta said, "A cinnamon owl. Spice in black chocolate."

He took a warm body of bread, ripped it open, and pulled out a handful of white flesh. He spread a soft, white butter formed in a round cake across the flesh of the bread, the flesh of flesh, and he dipped it into the remnant of cooked blood, animal juice, and spice. He packed this into his mouth and washed it down with another glass of wine.

Gabriella watched Simeon eat before she placed several small portions on her plate. Augusta ladled clear broth into a bowl, and with a glance toward Gabriella, she took a straw and began to drink.

When the first sips and bites were finished, and Gabriella had taken a sip of wine, Augusta said, "We must say whatever it is that we must say, in the wake of our father's death."

Gabriella's face was hard and the upper row of her perfect teeth gleamed unnaturally over the flesh of her lower lip. Augusta seemed to Simeon more translucent with each sip of her clear broth. He bent his head over his plate and met his food halfway while turning his head back and forth between bites, first toward Augusta, and then toward Gabriella, and then back toward Augusta.

His face was nearly in his food, and his belly spread

out beneath the table. "What are we supposed to talk about?"

Augusta answered, "Consummation. I want to talk about consummation."

"Consummation?" Simeon said past the bundle of carrots. He folded a white asparagus past his lips and spooned in some of the surprising ham-based hollandaise sauce accompanying it. "That is the climax of your visit?"

"Oh good god," Gabriella said. She took out her phone, made a call, and began to mumble instructions about her jet.

Augusta said, "I can't make the conversation go where it must go. Only Gabriel can do that."

Gabriella held the phone against her chest. "Stop calling me that."

Simeon took a large bite of mushroom gruyere. "Do we have to wait for Gabriella to figure out the point you are trying to make with all of this?"

Augusta nodded.

Simeon drank down another glass of wine. He sloshed wine onto his dirty undershirt as he refilled his glass. "All right then. Marvelous, in fact."

Gabriella closed her cell phone. "I will be leaving soon. We need to finish this."

"It is finished," Augusta said. "It was finished before you got here. It was finished the last week of your father's life, after I told him about you."

Simeon, full of tannin from the barrel-aged wine, interjected, "So, are you our lover, our sister, our guest, or our spouse?" His words were slurring, and they were muffled by the food crammed into his mouth.

Gabriella said, "Simeon, I want you come with me. Be my business partner. I will show you what you can do with the money. You can have as much time as you want to write your book or whatever you plan to do."

Simeon looked up. "Ah, brother, I already have that."

Gabriella's face did not soften, but it did seem momentarily genuine in a new way. "I need you. We will be partners. You will see new worlds. But I have to know tonight. Everything depends on you calling the Stump and undoing the damage that this liar has caused."

A spontaneous pause hovered in the air for a moment and the only sounds were those of eating, drink, the sea, and the voices of the kids on the beach. "I have been working on a little treatise to finish up my doctorate."

"From an actual university?"

Simeon briefly marveled at his brother's ability, without any facts, to hone in on the place that would cause most pain. "When I finish do you want to read it? After that I will discuss this partnership you speak of."

Gabriella reached the end of her apparent patience. She stood up. "Is there anything, at all, ever, that someone might suggest, that would be drearier than that?

"I have been working on notes for it all day." He pulled out a small stack of notecards that he had wrapped with a rubber band, and he felt a certain satisfaction at the modest weight of the stack. "If you promise to read it, I will seriously weigh your request and desires in the balance. Shall I?"

Gabriella rolled her eyes and sat down again.

"Well?"

She flung her hand into the air and dropped it back into her lap. "Just give me your notecards. I will imagine the rest. Simeon, everything depends on finishing this now."

"No, I must first write the book. It is for my Doctor of Immortality degree." The words did not feel like a confession. They felt like an assertion of all that his life had come to mean. "I must enlist the memory of our father, and LW, and LW's father, just to help me carry the tale. It will be a treatise about money, a speech about gods, a judgment about European and American history, a confession about our grandfather and the great Saint-Simone family. It will be a speech about your internet. It will be a treatise on the excess of freedom. My book will be called, *Angst, In Horrid Quiet*. It's a ridiculous idea, but I want to tell you about it."

"Well?"

Simeon took off the rubber band and shuffled through his notecards. "So, it will be about the religion of 'capitalism', which is the anagram of 'I am plastic.'"

"Simeon, please, for god's sake come to some point."

"Maybe I should have Jerome summarize my notecards for you."

"Simeon!"

Simeon looked down at the notecards in his hand. "I am on to something, Gabriella. I just know it. The money will help me finish my life work and take care of Augusta."

Augusta shook her head, no, but still said nothing.

Gabriella said, "Your Garden of Memory, your Theater, this wretched woman you say you care about ..." Her voice was thick with the frustration of knowing that without the money she would be ruined, and that indeed, Simeon had both the power to ruin her and, apparently, the light-hearted inclination to do so. "With your heart and your head wealth will be hell. You will kill yourself. You won't be able to endure it!"

"There is a strength that is enough to endure everything," Simeon felt a cold smile erupt from a place that he had never felt before. "The strength of the Saint-Simones. The strength of the Saint-Simone baseness. Everything is lawful." He looked at her in silence.

"Simeon." Gabriella's voice was resolute, with nothing dramatic in the tone. "If you intend to ruin me you should know that my life is at stake. I know the money will crush you. Give me the money and both of us can live."

"I am not ruining you. I have ideas for how to help America, and I need the money." Simeon looked around the table. "I need something with a bone. Something bigger than a fish bone." The food seemed to multiply magically.

Augusta handed him a turkey leg, baked and basted.

"I intend to stay here and marry Augusta," he said just before he bit into the roasted turkey leg, and caught a piece of cartilage that he chewed noisily. As his mouth noises from the animal he chewed grew, he knew the wildness of confession, which exploded the constriction of his clothes, of his solitude, of his walls. He swallowed, and bit again ferociously into the turkey leg, and allowed the grease on his chin to remain in defiance of … "Of nothing at all!" he said aloud.

"Nothing at all?" Gabriella sneered.

"I cannot," Augusta said firmly.

"Why not?" Simeon reached for three cinnamon owls. He did not eat them. He put them on the table at his elbow.

"Because," Gabriella answered for her, "she is mine."

Simeon wiped the turkey grease onto his undershirt. "Have you asked her?"

"No," Gabriella answered. "She asked me."

Simeon put down his gnawed-upon turkey leg. He did not believe his brother, she whose feet were wrapped in the skins of snakes. "Augusta? Is this true?"

Augusta shrugged. "Not in so many words. That was years ago. There is a force bigger than any of us working here."

"I am the force greater than yourself," Gabriella said.

Everyone seemed suddenly aware that for the first time Gabriella's so-called force was nearly spent, and she had no power over either of them. There was some scratching of plates, mostly from Simeon's fork, in the ensuing silence.

Augusta said, "We are here to honor our father."

Gabriella stood and reached for the ashes of her father and shook them. "Do you think I came to this dumping ground for a funeral dinner? Think! What would make me come here? The old man betrayed me. If there are rules, they are rules I make for myself." She unzipped her pants and pulled them down, revealing the scars from her sex-change operation. Then she urinated into the mason jar. Simeon and Augusta watched her. She replaced the cap and sloshed it around, looking at the yellow fluid and the gray ashes mingling.

Augusta said, "Is that your solution to the problem of the fortune?"

"Is marriage your solution to the problem of what you call the rape?"

Simeon said, "What rape?"

Still glaring at Augusta, Gabriella snapped back, "The story of the mythical rape is always told by the mortal, not the god. Let the god once tell you how things are and ..."

Augusta reddened. She whispered, or hissed, "No. My solution is forgiveness, not marriage."

"You were the one who lured me, damn you." Gabriella slammed her fist down on the table. "How many porn movies did you star in before you took up with my father?"

"Our father," she said.

"How many?"

"Twelve."

"Damn you. And damn you, Simeon. Damn you both."

Simeon watched through the veil of alcohol as he felt the house transforming into a theater of memory that drew its fire from the very heart of the cosmic conflict of fertility, gods, incest, fate. But the veil was not so thick as to hide the things that were coming into being. He asked again, feeling the pity of his state, "What rape?" He sat back and lit a cigarette. But it was not with satisfaction. Rather, it was a quizzical lighting. He smoked for a moment and lifted his father's ashes and looked through them, toward the moon, swirling them around, feeling the warmth of his brother's urine. "Is this our father?"

"It doesn't matter," Gabriella said.

"Is Augusta our sister?"

"It doesn't matter," she said again.

"What rape?"

"It doesn't matter," Gabriella grunted.

"This is not a satisfying catechism," Simeon said, like a man feeling around for a weapon and finding only a water pistol. "Almost everything matters, and this perhaps more than most things."

"You don't know her Simeon."

"You are the one who doesn't know me," Augusta answered. When Gabriella grunted again Augusta flinched. "I was pregnant. I carried the baby for weeks before I lost it. You ruined me. Even eating food is an unbearable mystery. Like sex. But things are being worked out inside me. Gabriel knows. If he didn't need the money he would have run away long ago."

Gabriella said, "See Simeon? Is this what you want to live with?"

Simeon answered. "Yes! I want to be stuck in the viscous muck of life. Oh sing the tadpole-like sperm wandering into the horns of the fallopian tubes where the ethereal ovum from that empyrean realm of the crystalline ovary, holding all the eggs that have been waiting, waiting, while sperm all over the world is generated by the trillions every day with genetic urgency … Hear me, searush, seamen, semen, Simeon. And how, brother, does money play against the cosmic tones of the drama about bringing forth a child?"

Gabriella wiped her mouth and put down her napkin. "Give me the money and I will leave. Forever."

Slowly Simeon realized that he was feeling rage for the first time in decades, and that the rage was coming over him at precisely his drunkest and most vulnerable moment when he could do nothing but strain to focus, closing one eye to keep from seeing double. How could the confession of rape come when he was least able to defend himself, least able to rise up and produce a real action, an authentic response that matched the crime? Ye gods, he was as bad off as the cuckold on Jerry Springer.

Every dish on the table had been ravaged by Simeon, and he was full and very drunk. And he was very unsettled. What did he want? He looked around the table and pulled out another cigarette. The platters were in disarray. Bones were piled up. The ashes of his father had settled to the bottom, and Gabriella's urine was cooling. Something was wrong. There was just a big mess, an uncomfortable fullness, and nothing was being finished. Jerome continued in sulky silence, sitting on the floor, wrapped up in his crossed arms and tucked chin.

Simeon did not light his cigarette immediately. He lifted one of the cinnamon owls beside his plate. The chocolate was dark, nearly black, and he knew it would be bitter. He bit into the owl. The inside was dark red, like congealed blood, almost solid, chewy. He held the bite in his mouth and began to hum as it melted, and only the residuum of spice and bitterness covered his tongue. He put the other half of the owl in his mouth, and chewed, and paused, and swallowed. "Let us each make a confession," he finally said. "Let us make things clean."

Gabriella sneered again.

Simeon lit his cigarette. He tried to speak without slurring his words. He felt a kind of spiritual vertigo. "Nothing good has come of this family. Confession is the last beacon, the last chance for something good. Confess, and I might give you the money."

"All right," Augusta said. "A confession then."

Gabriella stood, sober, hard as marble. "Of what? To whom?"

Simeon thought that in this moment he saw something singular about his powerful brother, something that would make her destruction horribly fascinating, like watching a high-rise building crash in on itself. Simeon was a seven-year-old boy crouching inside a nearly four-hundred-pound body, watching from far away, and he thought from this great distance he might even be willing to die at his brother's hand just to move in close enough to the torrent that was his brother's world, close enough to catch a glimpse. Gabriella was towering now, and the faintest appearance of hesitation bloomed again like light on a bubble.

Simeon tumbled on. "I confess that I am in love with Augusta. I do not even care if she is my half-sister."

"She is not our sister," Gabriella said. This sounded like a topic of which she had grown weary.

"I might be. Your father raped my mother many years before I met him. Why is it not possible that we are family?"

"Why do you want us to be?"

When no one else confessed anything, Simeon reached over to the jar of ashes and looked at the urine. He held up the jar. "What is your confession Gabriella?"

"I am leaving," she answered.

"More."

"Tonight I will be financially ruined."

Simeon shook his head. "More." Simeon lit his cigarette, and drew in a great breath through the straw of tobacco, and let the smoke cover the platters like a fog in a cemetery.

Augusta lifted the eggshell of her head and pulled out one of the tulips which she began to pluck. Finally she said, "I put some of your father's ashes into the food I prepared."

Gabriella whispered, "You are an abomination. Take stock Simeon. She will ruin you too."

"It is not true Simeon. I did not seduce him. I did nothing more than live in his general vicinity at a time when he felt like taking something. I did not steal the money. When he found out about Gabriel, your father gave the money to me as the only penance he knew how to achieve. But I am a penitent myself, so I don't want riches."

Gabriella said, "She craves nothing more than for a god to descend and impregnate her."

"You are my horror, Gabriel. I am not the one who told your father."

Simeon glanced at Jerome who sat on the floor, but no helpful interpretations or quips came from the sullen man. Simeon closed one eye to keep Jerome in focus.

Just then, the Cuban let his hands drop from his chest to his side, and blood ran down his shirt and pants. Simeon was aware that his own calm register of the observation was probably not appropriate, but alcohol and weariness have a strange effect on the mind of man.

"I know that," Gabriella said, lowering her upturned hand to the Cuban. "You want a confession, Simeon? This is my confession. For several years this man ran our father's library. He stayed mostly hidden, but he was the only witness to this so-called rape in the library. He is the one who told our father."

When Simeon's soul misfired on the edge of faith, as it always did, he would usually lie on his tilt-table watching the perfect young women below, and he would dwell on the possibility that some measure of what Aquinas must have felt in his world of form and purpose would manifest itself in one of his own future great works: *The Critique of Practical Irony* or *Tractatus Ironius Practicalus*. He had slurped at the philosophical trough, feeding on the thin gruel of refutation, or the thinner gruel of professional gain at such efforts. He needed more.

Simeon Saint-Simone, A.B.D., thought he had been redeemed when he stumbled across the idea of his Garden of Memory, something worthy of a life of work. And one day—so went the larger vision—he would rise up in the midst of his great solitude. He would take pen and paper, and bending forward, flesh hanging from his great and mighty skull, cigarette perched precariously on his lip, he would write the first sentence. Thus would his personal apocalypse resolve into a hymn of praise for his own immortality, masked as a critique of waste and transience. And it would, of course, end with a last sentence by which he would stand or fall. Ah, the lure of immortality.

But now he knew that if Augusta left, he would again

be nothing more than a mind lodged somewhere atop a massive and unhealthy body, planning his Garden of Memory in an aimless and meandering way. Suddenly his groggy imagination formed an unexpected place to center this world, an alien *topos*—Augusta's womb, the tethering place to a new reality.

Was he not an obese, solitary, middle-aged man? And yet everything lingered in the moment, confirming the perfect fit of their phagocentric philosophies. Her womb floated on the edge of the world of his thought like a moon.

She could not know. She had lived with her body her entire life. Her familiar world was his alien world. So with everyone. His solitude had made him privy to the strangeness of the familiar. That! That was the missing ingredient. And it was lodged there in that small, moist, dark, periodically succulent place so far removed from the consciousness that had occupied all his works and days. Though this might be the great impossibility of his life, there was no logical obstacle to him planting a part of himself in that alien world, and having a new human being grow.

These were thoughts accessible only to a middle-aged virgin male. But was there yet another secret? Was isolation from familiarity the secret to retaining insight into magic, faith, joy, animism, theism, or whatever? Insight into the presence of something other than the facts in the world? Was this the secret of the monks, nuns and saints? Was this the argument for the celibacy of the priests? Was this the key to memory and forgetfulness? Was denial the key to such unfamiliarity, and unfamiliarity the key to holiness? To seeing the holy? Unfamiliarity. Unfamilial. Was this what Christ meant when he said to hate one's family? His mind tumbled lightly across a place of infinite depth.

In the moment his thoughts, which had no mass, distributed themselves evenly throughout his massive body and yielded a pleasurable fear. No longer would he think of himself as some culmination or cultural aberration. Instead of summarizing his small version of the universe in a book which would be stillborn, Simeon Saint-Simone was to be a part of humanity, a potential continuation of the human story. All doubt was to be swept away in this new and utterly unfamiliar thought: the resolution of his many questions would find its singular and wordless origin in Augusta, whether in her womb, or her hunger, or her infinite denial. He had no idea.

He was no longer a seeker of wisdom, alone. He had

parted ways with Socrates and was to become an evangelist of unwritten, unironic life.

"My God," Simeon blurted out, his tongue thick with alcohol, just as Jerome the Cuban rose to a kneeling position on the floor. "I think I am cured of philosophy!"

Jerome pushed himself further up and reclined against the cabinets. "I am sorry Augusta."

"For what?" she asked.

Jerome's voice was strained with agony. "Gabriella, did you shoot me to kill me, or to forget?"

"I shot your lion, not you. Even the lion only got a scratch. Why didn't you just leave my father's house? Why insist on destroying me because of your rules?"

"The rules don't belong to me."

"Well, they're not mine either. I will not live by them." Gabriella looked away. "I am leaving. Simeon, I will not beg. But know this. I am unshackled. I am cast down. You know to be wary of a fallen angel."

Jerome the Cuban called out, "May I have last rites?"

"I told you, it's just a scratch," Gabriella said again. She turned to Augusta. "The gods will have what the gods will have. Admit the thrill of being taken."

"How dare you," she answered.

"I must have last rites," the Cuban cried out. "I will repent of both sins. Of all sins."

"Maybe you can repent of original sin and be done with it," Gabriella snarled. Then she leaned toward Simeon and whispered in his ear. "Your precious Dante needed his precious Beatrice to be dead if she was going to be of any use to him."

Simeon said with a numb tongue, "So the spirit of philosophy has left me and passed into the well-swept and empty bins of my brother, and finding much room there has brought seven like spirits with it."

Gabriella's cell phone rang. She mumbled for a moment. "Think, Simeon. Don't let this whore and this celibate voyeur distract you from the wisdom of a partnership with me. The money is mine, but we are brothers. Don't reject your brother. This opportunity will never come again."

Simeon rose up in theatrical confidence and announced, "No!" as though the only consequence to his words would be the scripted response of the fellow actor. But then he watched the woman who was his brother step over the bleeding Cuban without another word, and he knew that she was bound by nothing.

"If I sign the money over to you, will you leave us alone?"

"Yes."

"Well I refuse!" He suddenly understood that he had either done the best thing in his life, or the most dangerous and deadly thing in his life, or perhaps both.

Augusta said, "Even if he gave it to you, Gabriel, you would never again have success that is your own, free of your brother's decision. Your success would always be his. If he gave you the money you would be something much worse—a failure forced to act like a success. You're a failure and a fake, and you will forever to be compared to your wildly successful father."

Gabriella looked stunned for a moment, and then she nodded. "You surprise, Augusta. You are crueler than even I suspected." She breathed loudly through her magnificent nose for a long, uncomfortable while. And then, she left the house without saying another word.

Jerome groaned, "I am guilty, I repent."

"You can only repent of the sin you are guilty of," Augusta said.

Simeon bubbled words past the molasses of his saliva. "Why are you talking about sin now? I want to continue the human race. I want to create human beings, souls, minds capable of producing whole worlds. And I want them to know who I am, and who you are. Marry me Augusta, and explain this later." He felt his huge dinner pressing up into his esophagus, and he washed it back down with a large swig from the bottle of wine. He held it toward Jerome the Cuban.

Jerome continued on in his mournful mantra. "I am guilty, I repent."

"Gabriel raped me. You only watched. They're different sins."

He looked at her with one eye squinted, the other with an open stare augmented by the arch of the raised eyebrow above it. "Are they?"

"We should probably call an ambulance," Augusta said.

With slurred disagreement Simeon said, "Sounds like he wants a priest instead."

Augusta knelt beside the Cuban. Simeon continued his statement from his dinner chair. "Do you realize that the human race might continue through the union of our two frailties?"

"You are so drunk, Simeon."

Simeon straightened himself and lit a cigarette. "There!" he said. "I sober up quickly. Listen, I am talking about immortality."

"Immortality is not a thing to be worked out inside my body."

"What do you mean? I want to have a child with you."

He carefully relocated to his tilt table.

"We have to take care of your Cuban."

Simeon started to blubber moistly. "No, but what do you mean?" In the silence he could hear his children on the beach laughing and laughing. He listened to them frolic as he felt his inverted ship try to upright itself. "I am alone while the world drips with fertility," he moaned.

She held a dishtowel to the wound in the side of Jerome the Cuban. "Not this part of the world. I don't even ovulate anymore."

Ovulate. He almost never thought of ovulation. "Then I shall be like the Castrati, forced into sterility, singing my little songs of grief until my death."

Augusta said, "Why do you always have to speak so strangely?"

"Finally a question I can answer! It's because of goddamned Socrates."

She looked at him with large eyes, and she stood and came close to him. He smelled the overwhelmingly desirable after-dinner breath of a functioning female human with the barely perceptible evidence of plaque on her kissable teeth belying a bacterial transience that

contrasted with the eternal feel of the potential of procreation and spiritual life.

So motivated, he said again with a cool, calm grumble, "Because of goddamned Socrates."

She bent down and kissed his lips gently, the first
kiss he had ever had.

"Oh, life," he sighed without a trace of philosophy
in the thought. He took a swig of wine, feeling the diz-
zying and delicious turmoil of the kiss that was a key,
unlocking a new world inside himself.

Augusta wiped away the blood from Jerome's belly,
and there was no wound. "So it was only blood from
the lion?"

"Maybe I was miraculously healed," Jerome speculated.

Through his blurry vision, down below, Simeon saw

the unmistakable silhouette of one of the lovely girls, dark against the glow of embers from the bonfire. Her shadow was turned slightly toward him. What was she looking at? Of course. She was staring at the enormous man lying at an angle in the soft light of his reading lamp sublimely illuminated, looking down upon them, an epiphany, an icon in the golden glow. How like a god he must look.

And how, he suddenly thought, like a dirty old man. She pointed toward him, and several others turned to look. Were they mumbling among themselves? Suddenly he was overwhelmed with embarrassment and the world filled in with pettiness like a gas. He reached over with some effort and turned out the light. Everything was darkness. He was ashamed and exposed. His tilt-table had become a veritable bier.

Simeon Saint-Simone was forty-nine, A.B.D. in philosophy, weighed almost 400 pounds, had met Presidents, and was richer than 99.9% of the entire world. How does one grow up? he suddenly wondered, like a prom reject in his senior year still pining after the girl who was prom-queen and who would distract his mind with its I.Q. of 165 for the rest of his imaginative life. How does one catch up with the body determined to grow old and die when so much remained to be accomplished?

Though he had turned out his own light, he was aware that the girl below still held out her hand, pointing. Then gradually light began to grow around her, and to illuminate her. In the fog of his vision she looked beatific. But where was the light coming from? Ah, he thought as he heard the drumming of an engine muffled over his roof. A helicopter. So perhaps she was not pointing at him. Perhaps he did not have to be embarrassed. But a helicopter?

Just then he saw eight police cars drive onto the beach, followed by the van from the television news crew he had watched so many times. They stopped by the bonfire. A satellite dish began to rise from the van as a young man in a suit stepped out and adjusted his coat and his hair while the camera man flicked on another light and prepared to report live for the nightly news.

With some effort he lifted his remote control and turned on the television.

There was the young man, making his career. "Thank you Linda. Earlier this evening a resident of this otherwise quiet beachside neighborhood reported hearing a gunshot. Your K-news-live-action-report-team has since learned from an anonymous source that a man named Simeon Saint-Simone is holding two people hostage inside, one of whom is wounded, possibly fatally. A neighbor said that Mr. Saint-Simone is an eccentric recluse who, in the neighbor's words, 'Is more damaging to property values than to life and limb.' Nonetheless, for this son of a wealthy businessman, it looks like he has had enough of solitude. We have not yet heard his demands. The SWAT team has surrounded the house and is preparing to start negotiations. We will be following this story closely through the evening. Another K-news-live-action report-team first-strike," and with the words "first strike" he punched the air, one two, and Simeon suddenly felt a wave of nausea. "Back to you Linda."

He turned off the television.

Two more gulps and the wine was finished. The bottle dropped to the ground. Simeon felt overwhelmed by the pull of sleep.

The phone rang.

His own gruff voice on the answering machine erupted into the air.

The annoying beep.

Then, "Simeon and Augusta. I am calling you from the jet. I see the camera crews have arrived. I thought this might make for a fine Kodak moment. If you look out your window, near the horizon, you might see my light. I am circling over the sea, and in a few minutes I will be flying toward you. You will soon be famous." She hung up.

Simeon's eyes grew very heavy. He was becoming confused. Did he or did he not hate Socrates?

With one eye shut Simeon looked around at the dust-covered, trashy belongings he had collected in his house and Garden, belongings that were supposed to encompass all of human memory. How he wished to tear away the veil. But what to do when the veil is human memory? What a narrow path. What a hard thing to be a conscious human being, to ride the swell formed by the crash of memory and the thing remembered, revelation and the question, philosophy and poetry. He was tired. His thought kept reverting to the same formulations, words and more words, never really getting at the thing. He let his mind enter the Theater of Memory, the place where he could always calm himself, the true Theater that was his mind, of which the wooden Theater was only a shadow. There he saw LW still reclining in one of the aisles, reading a detective magazine. And on the stage was Camillo.

"I am going out," Simeon announced. "I am going through the door and down to the Garden. We have got to get out of here."

"Out of where?" Augusta said.

"It doesn't matter. We have to climb out."

"Fine, then. Go!"

"I am going. Please come with me. Please."

And with an unsteady gait, Simeon lifted his massive body and walked toward the door. He turned the handle and stepped out into the darkness, into the breeze, into the fresh smell of the ocean and the delicious residuum of the smoky bonfire. He opened the back door and stepped forward onto the landing, and the day's alcohol, and the food, and the grief, and the infinite sky lightened his head, and he heard laughter from his twin and Camillo and LW and all who have, in the history of humanity, had great falls. All of humanity laughed. The glow of the embers, and the stars, and the helicopter's beam, and the lights of the news truck, and the Christmas lights all around his Garden of Memory began to swirl, and the vortex of the swirling lights formed a passage through which he might go, and he felt himself losing his balance so that there was, at long last, no choice, and then he began to fall down the steps, the great cycle coming around again, he fell, sliding, fell, with a fall like being born, born again. And he fell and fell and his mass pulled forward like the waves lapping toward the moon, and he fell and rolled and landed at the bottom breathless, unsure whether his breath was knocked out of him, or whether the pain he now felt in his neck meant that his spinal cord had been severed and he was dying. Either seemed fine in the moment.

From where his eyes and mind rested he could see the mountain of his belly rise up. But he lay ever so still. All around him glowed the Christmas lights making the Garden of Memory seem suddenly magical, finished. Jerome the Cuban had added the missing ingredient. Light. Just then his injured lion came close and sat beside him and licked his face.

Looking up at the stars, past the lion's mane, he could see the window through which he had taken in the world. And he supposed the cure was complete. But he did not know exactly what that meant.

This was no time for questions. Here was something new. He had tasted it before, long ago when he was just a boy. Now, suddenly he was surprised by the feeling of an old and invisible presence whom he could not name. This was the time to be silent, as he felt the breath of the lion against his face. And in that silence he heard the distant roar of his brother's jet. The sound gradually grew louder, mingling with the pounding of the helicopter and the screams of scattering youth all documented by the young news reporter in a suit.

He lay still looking up, feeling a profound wonder overcome his body and his fatigue.

The young people began to say things loudly and then to gasp and to scream as the low flying jet came closer and the roar grew deafening.

But there he was, a piece of debris among pieces of debris, and he was tasting something which he did not want to name just yet. This was his start, this thing recollected from youth, wonder, this sense of a friend, friendly. For once he did not need to name anything.

He lay listening and looking up, feeling a great peace, filling up with longing beneath the lovely ancient stars, the dying lion licking his face.

The ever-faithful Jerome appeared at the top of the steps and began to descend.

The jet roared in with moonlight illuminating its ghostly covering. And the ground began to shake. Gabriella must have been flying the machine ten feet above the water toward Simeon's home. The roar became unbearable, like the beginnings of new lands in the earthquake, or when the mighty Spirit hovering over the deep decides it is time for the land and the water to separate. And then the airplane roared over him, and it seemed to be moving very slowly, and Simeon felt the lion lift his head and look up. The jet flew straight up into the sky, circled, and headed away over the ocean, just above the waves. Soon it skimmed the water and tumbled to stillness.

Just then a final thought occurred to Simeon, a beautiful thought. Aristotle once speculated that the stars, as they move on their paths, make music. The universe sang love, sang through starlight that all shall be well, and all manner of things shall be very well. Simeon suddenly knew, as his own vision dimmed, and then dimmed further, and he felt rising inside himself an ecstasy of complete and utter lightness, as though his body was fading away, and his lean soul was finally free, that in this Aristotle was closer to the truth than in almost anything else he said. Not lofty speech, nor a mere absence of sound, but music, with long, meaningful silences between the wailing notes.

RAYMOND BARFIELD is a writer and physician. He has published several books of philosophy, poetry, and fiction. *The Seventh Sentence* is his second novel.